The Unicorn Hunter

Written by: Del Henderson

Illustrated by: Del Henderson Jr.

GEMOO Publishing

ISBN - 13: 978-0692614648

‒ DEDICATION ‒

Dedicated to my little cousins Morgan, Kaitlyn, Emily, and Audrey who were so adamant about me writing a story for them about unicorns. So like any good evil cousin I made a twist on their most beloved creature to show that all is not always as it seems. Please sit back and enjoy as this humble tale of woe unfolds, and may it not prove distasteful to those who wish to read it.

- CONTENTS -

- CHAPTER ONE -

THE LONG, NOT-SO-FORGOTTEN PAST

Listen and be warned of a secret of past,
these warnings of a hunter to the hunted do not pass.
Creature baptized by night's chrisom sheet,
pray for your soul that eyes do not meet.
The shrieking neigh of a foe of old,
shall not bode well for it has been foretold.
When pale death gallops by,
a mortal's time is always nigh.
Hide those, whose souls are fresh,
else it shall turn to lament.
Learn the sign of the leaves divine,
this so pale death may pass you by.
Creature of the night disguised as from the sun,
shall try to make humanity undone.
If one is to avoid the gaping maw,
then remove the source of its song.

Poetry: rarely is there something more mysterious, beautiful, or entertaining to the mind. Poems, no matter if they be dark in nature or light, are truly marvelous, for within their words they have messages of wisdom that ought to be listened to. History, of course, shows more than naught that people just read them, thinking them nice before going on to the next of the poems' brethren, skimming through the wisdom of the past without even a pause or second glance. These words, which proud men read to impress those around them, never thinking of the meanings inside of them-these words! Wretched are the ones who are not aware of their warnings and doom is upon their brow as it was upon mine, for I, too, mistook their purpose and was struck by the plague called insolence. These words, which are bound in leather flesh, which men find so easy to disregard shall prove to be their salvation in the end. The warnings now to me are very clear, but in the beginning of this tale they were not and so my gloomy fate had been set.

My name is Jack Tanner and I was for some time a small town lawyer in the humble state of Illinois. The life that I had carved out for my family was not a glamorous one. We had just enough income to get us by, but that was fine by us, for we were happy in each other's company. At first there were the three of us: my wife Rachel, my daughter Abigail, and myself. That was, of course, before the cancer. It took a full year for the good Lord to call Rachel home, for she was a stubborn woman and my inspiration. To say that I took her death hard would be an understatement; for a time all that I could do was curse the world and linger on Rachel's memories through the empty bottles of whiskey which littered the floor before the old television. To my eternal shame, there were even times that I forgot about Abigail, my only daughter, my little princess. Abigail looked very much like her mother with flowing blond hair and radiant blue eyes that could pierce even a cloudy day, and the Lord knows that I had many of them. If I was more aware of what was happening around her I could have done something; I wish…I wish that I had, but the realization of my mistakes came too late.

One thing must be made clear, a warning if you will. When darkness clouds a man's soul, it calls to dark things, evil things that thrive on these ill vibes. These creatures, if they can even be called that, will not show themselves as they feed and one is only aware of their presence when and only when they have had their fill. This said; don't linger in the darkness of the mind for it will only bring pain.

My story begins over a year ago. I had lost my job and the house was soon to follow. It was truly a dark time in my life. The atmosphere of what used to be my lovely home was very bleak. Whether this was caused by the drafts which came from its dis-repaired walls or the horror that was to come, I know not. However, one thing is certain the house since my wife's passing seemed empty and alone…so alone. Its dark interior was like a black void of painful memories so strong that it seemed the surrounding fields even lost some of their color when their roots ventured too close to the lonely house. Somehow it seemed fit to be so, as to match the rugged look of the wooden house's frame with its lopsided window shutters, peeling paint, cracked windows, it's tall yard comprised of dandelions, poison ivy, clover, all kinds of weedy flowers, and of course grass. For I did not mow it; no, I didn't see the point to mowing. Anywhere the yard wanted to go was fine by me and I was more than content to let the house forever be lost in its undergrowth away from the prying eyes of the world. To be forgotten seemed best to me, to be a long lost page of sorrow of the world's history forgotten in the vastness of time like all other sad tales of woe.

The fog of despair was indeed very thick in my mind during that time. So lost was I that sometimes unknowingly in intoxicated fits of rage I would dare to even harm the precious golden hair of my poor little Abigail. I curse that time, for such a poor father was I, never can I forgive myself for the harm I did to my little girl who was suffering just as much as I. If the good Lord would permit it, I would give up anything, even my own life just to take back what I had done. I was in a dark place and as I told you before, when darkness clouds a man's soul, it calls to evil things, nasty things.

I remember the first hint of its coming very well. The corn had just begun to grow in my neighbor's fields where little Abigail used to play and the night was coming on fast, leaving a red fiery sunset in the darkening sky.

Of course, I paid little heed to it. The T.V. was on and I for the most part just stared with glassy eyes at its surface. I know not what was on and didn't care; it was white noise, a distraction from what was around me as I sat in my worn down ripped and stained, filthy recliner. It could be said that strange things had happened in the house before, but until this time they could be explained away with some imagination, but not this one. As I sat drinking a bottle like a newborn baby would, for it was my only comfort, I heard it. The noise was very much like a dark, slightly musical whisper that creaked through the house's joists. Mind you, the whisper didn't say anything recognizable but somehow I knew that in it were all the answers that a mortal man would care to know. The noise drifted first from the attic then to the second floor, then to the first where I was sitting in shadows. Shortly after it came upon the first floor, it dissipated towards the basement. Even though I was drunk at the time I still remember clearly with dread, the heavy and intoxicating pressure which befell the house that day, and the days after.

     The gloomy atmosphere, however, didn't seem to affect Abigail at all. In fact, it seemed to have brightened her little face and give her more energy when she would play out in the fields, which only helped convince me that the gloom was in my own head. Even when objects started to move on their own and eerie sounds could be heard in the late hours of night, she still had a brave and cheerful face. I even remember how she would come to me, beaming, while asking that I play with her and her imaginary friend Summer to which I would always respond that I was not in the mood to play children's games. What a fool I was! If I had known that just a few weeks later she would be taken from me I would have spent all the time I could have with her.

As you may have guessed, my little Abigail is gone. One night I woke up in my chair during the early hours just before morning. Having spilled a drink on myself while asleep, I slowly got up and headed upstairs to change clothes. As I made my way down the hall I peeked into Abigail's room, but to my horror, she was not there. Frantically, I left the house in a desperate search, calling to her with every step I took. It was raining and I could barely see anything in front of me but still I searched, becoming more frantic with every minute that passed. With a shaky voice that only became shakier, I called to Abigail as the mud began to suck onto my boots, as if deliberately trying to impede my search but it did not stop me. When I finally found her she was lying next to our neighbor's old horse corral's wooden fence, dead. I don't know how long I knelt beside her wailing and letting loose so many tears that the rain storm itself was put to shame. But when my body finally dried up and no more tears could come, I slowly picked up my precious little girl and turned around, catching a glimpse of a white horse in the corral before carrying her away.

The next few months after that, I lost all the will to live, I simply lost everything: my wife, my daughter, and the house which was being foreclosed. Life had no meaning for me anymore and I cursed God for letting it happen. I still don't understand why it happened, but the blame I know now was my own, not His. The doctor had put me on anti-depressants when my first suicide attempt failed and put me in the hospital for a week. The medicine helped but only very little, for no amount of drugs could replace the void in me. I will not bore you with the details of that time but will tell you that if there was a hell on Earth, that was it. When I had to pack my late wife's and daughter's belonging before the house was foreclosed, the memories and pain that came were just too much to bear. Though nothing struck me with more grief than when I found Abigail's diary. When I read how she observed my depression since her mother's death and her plans to cheer me up, I choked on my own sorrow. The last few entries, though, were different than the pages before, for these had to deal with Summer, her imaginary friend. I will tell you now what they said, for I carefully studied them and now know them by heart.

Entry 405

Dear Diary, today I had met a wonderful new friend in the neighbor's yard. He said that his name is Summer. We played and he showed me many wonderful things, I hope to play with him again tomorrow!

Entry 406
Dear Diary, Summer taught me about the beauty of the flower and how they bring happiness to those who see them. I think that tomorrow I will bring some home for daddy to cheer him up.

Entry 407
Dear Diary, Today Summer gave me a ride on his back! We went really fast and even jumped over a bush! I really liked it. Summer said that he could even fly like a bird and some-day will take me through the sky. I'm not so sure about this for heights kind of scare me.

Entry 408
Dear Diary, today daddy yelled at me for making too much noise and made me cry. However Summer cheered me up and said that daddy was just angry because mommy had to leave us and that he still loved me. This made me happy again.

Entry 409
Dear Diary, met Summer again today at our usual spot which he calls a horse corral, that makes sense because he is a horse!

Entry 410
Dear Diary, I was mistaken yesterday and Summer correct-ed me, he is a unicorn not a horse. Imagine that I'm friends

with a real unicorn!

Entry 411
Dear Diary, today I told Summer about my field trip to
Springfield last year, he seemed very interested. He also
showed me how to brush his white coat that was fun. He's
like a giant doll!

Entry 412
Dear Diary, sorry I didn't write the last two days but I was
very sick. I wanted to see Summer but daddy made me stay
in bed.

Entry 413
Dear Diary, I told Summer why I didn't see him the last
three days and he said that its just normal for little girls
to get sick from time to time. He also told me about his
magical world. They have grass made of chocolate, soda
fountains, balloons, all the candy I could ever want, fluffy
animals including kitties, I always wanted a kitten. His
world sounds amazing and someday I would like to visit it.

Entry 414
Dear Diary, today Summer told me that he wants to take me
to his world!

Entry 415
Dear Diary, I was sick again but I was able to visit Summer

today to play.

Entry 416
Dear Diary, I couldn't write yesterday because I was sick in bed. I hope to be able to visit Summer tomorrow.

Entry 417
Dear Diary, Summer said that I would be ready soon to travel to his world, I can't wait!

Entry 418
Dear Diary, I was sick again today, I hope it passes soon. Daddy told me that I should take it easy and stay in bed today so I was not able to see Summer.

Entry 419
Dear Diary, I was able to play with Summer today! We had lots of fun.

Entry 420
Dear Diary, today I woke up woozy and the room was spinning so I did not go outside today but tomorrow I will visit Summer.

Entry 421
Dear Diary, Summer told me that I am ready to go to his world, I can't wait to taste the cotton candy bushes!

Tomorrow morning we are going to leave. I will leave a note on the fridge to tell daddy where I went so he doesn't worry.

There were no more entries in her diary and when I checked the old stained fridge the note was not there. I could not make any sense of it: Abigail's last entries were confusing to say the least. I knew that she was sick the last few days before her death but I never imagined it to have caused such hallucinations. I also never dreamed that she would have died from the illness either, but that's what the doctor said happened. I opened the fridge to grab another beer, which was the only thing it was stocked with, but as I did I saw a corner of a stained white paper sticking out from underneath the fridge. Upon investigation I found it to be the note from Abigail.

Dear daddy, do not worry for I went with Summer to his world.
Summer is a white unicorn and my best friend.
He told me that I will be back soon so don't worry.
I love you, Abigail.

I don't know why, but the note sent a shiver down my spine. That note was written the day she died and it sounded like she knew she was going away. It couldn't be that she committed suicide and the doctor was mistaken, could it? She seemed so happy and what about Summer? I am sure that a psychologist would simply say that it was her subconscious telling her in a form of a hallucination that she was going to die soon. That excuse, however, couldn't be, for my neighbor Timothy O'Conel had a white horse. I saw it the very night Abigail died…but still, even though it was masked in the rain it did seem to have something long on its forehead and didn't the creature have a soft glow about it? No, that was impossible! It was a regular horse, had to be. Besides, I was too old to believe in such nonsense.

Time, however, would prove me wrong. After I had sent the house's stuff to a storage container until I could find a new home, I found myself inspecting the old horse corral on Timothy's land. It was well made, and even though time had worn its wood planks and molded some of the oak posts, the fence was solid.

"What are you doing here, Jack?" my neighbor asked me from behind, making me jump.

I turned around, looking at the elderly gentleman with his worn cowboy hat. Timothy was the very definition of a country man with his cowboy boots, cowboy shirt, and even a cowboy mustache which was a pepper grey. He listened to country music from his beat up silver truck, which was made in America, of course. "Just taking a last look before I leave," I replied.

Timothy stuck his hands into his blue jean pockets. "I am sorry to hear about your daughter," he said moving closer.

"Yep," was all I could say, trying my best to keep

my emotions under control.

"So this is where you found her?" he asked.

"Yep."

"I know she loved this spot. Used to play here all the time," Timothy stated, looking out into the un-kept corral.

"Yep," I replied, "she did like your horse."

Timothy stared at me with a puzzled expression. "What horse?"

"You know, the white one."

"There has not been a horse in this place for about 15 years, Jack."

That was what I was hoping not to hear. Timothy must have seen that I was troubled and asked if I was all right, to which I lied "Yep" then walked away to my beat up black truck. I quickly got in and drove away. I had no idea what to do. I knew that I saw the white horse…unicorn, whatever it was. Abigail's diary and note didn't leave much room for any other conclusion. The mere fact that I saw it at the exact location it always met her and then read about the creature in Abigail's diary was too much to be a coincidence. I had to learn more, there was something not right with all this and I was going to find out what it was, if not for my own peace of mind, then for Abigail.

The first place that I began looking was the library. Being an old-fashioned guy I preferred a book to the blinding screen of a computer, in which half of the information that can be found comes from unreliable sources. Even in court a book will likely have more of an influence than a document on the web. I spent many weeks reading and studying everything related to horses or mythical creatures, and by the time the books started to repeat themselves, I had become quite an expert on the matter. I might have even been able to perform surgery on any of the creatures if it was truly necessary. The librarian, Peggy, was quite helpful and only stared at me questionably when I checked out the books on unicorns from the children's section. Those books, it can be said, were no help at all; they were all puffy clouds and rainbows. Many of the stories on unicorns were happy and not threatening in any way, but what can one expect from a children's book? However, there was something very odd about the stories, something familiar, but I just couldn't put my finger on it. Unicorns were creatures of light, good in their nature, and seemed to interact with children because of their imaginations. If the creatures really did exist it would be natural for them to prefer interactions with children for their imaginations would allow them to be more accepting of them. Even in the few mythological books where unicorns were mentioned they were good and could not cause harm. But that left me with a very serious question: if that was truly a unicorn then what happened to my Abigail? Was I really just seeing things in the rainy darkness after all? The more I researched, the more I doubted what I saw, for there was no proof other than a few old myths that unicorns really existed.

I pondered these questions as I entered my

apartment in a run-down neighborhood. The streets were dirty and littered with heaps of trash which sometimes concealed winos who would tug at coats, begging for money as people passed on their way home. The apartment was small and drafty, many of the walls had cracks running up them that an occasional cockroach would use to enter the room. The room had a small noisy refrigerator and a moldy sink for a kitchen, and a mat on the floor for a bed which smelled of something terrible. It was not like the house I was living in before, but it was cheap and did not constantly remind me of the life that I once had. There was no bathroom in the unit but instead it was located down the building's dimly lit hall, shared by five other units. My neighbors, thankfully, kept to themselves. They seemed to be members of the rougher side of life, and if they were investigated I would not be the least bit surprised to learn that some of them were escaped convicts. I myself must have not looked much better, for they seemed to have accepted me into their world with grunts of dissatisfaction when we happened to pass each other in the hall. Nobody had to worry about thievery in that apartment complex; there was nothing to steal. That said, there was also no reason to get to know anyone, so content was I with the ceremonial exchange of grunted greetings in the morning with my neighbors. The apartment was cheap and cost very little to rent. Obviously the owner was using the property's lack of income as a loss on his taxes, but I cared not, for more pressing concerns were weighing on my mind.

When I entered my apartment, I sat down on the only chair I had, which was little more than a stool, and poured some cereal into a bowl, being careful to pick out the cockroaches that fell into the yellow-stained dish from the box, before digging into my supper. The room was dimly lit, for the only source of light was a single light bulb hanging from the ceiling by a wire. This light source cast many an eerie shadow across the room and onto my weight bench, which was the only real piece of furniture I had, and used it I did. In fact, the reason that I am so muscular today can be traced from that time of lifting weights while thinking about what I had read in the library. I wish you could have seen me before that time; I was more of a stick than a man. It's interesting how time changes a person.

I didn't have a clock to tell me what time it was nor a television to watch, for these were just distractions to my main goal. The mystery of the unicorn had to be unraveled in order to discover two things. The first was to determine whether or not my little Abigail was murdered by some un-natural thing, and the second was to find out the condition of my own sanity. I didn't have any other pressing matters to attend to, and since the rent of the apartment was so low, I could stay there for many years and not have to work. This was essential so I could focus my entire being into the mission I had given myself.

When the library started to run dry with infor-mation, I turned to the internet and even asked random strangers online about any encounters with unicorns they may have had. They mostly responded quite rudely and were of no help. In truth I had nearly given up the search when one day, by mere chance, I picked up a most peculiar book on Latin poems of the 15th century. The book was actually from my Latin class when I attended college. I searched for so long in libraries, internet sites, bookstores, even paintings and the key to the mystery was in my possession all along! Isn't that ironic? Of course I didn't know it was the key to the mystery at the time and when I found it in my old gym bag when visiting the storage unit, I put off reading it for several weeks. It took some time to refresh my Latin before any of its mysteries could be made out. One particular poem by a man named Jonathan Kipling caught my full attention.

Listen and be warned of a secret of past, these warnings of a hunter to the hunted do not pass.

Creatures baptized by night's chrisom sheet, pray for your soul that eyes do not meet.

The shrieking neigh of a foe of old, shall not bode well for it has been foretold.

When pale death gallops by, a mortal's time is always nigh.

Hide those, whose souls are fresh, else it shall turn to lament.

Learn the sign of the leaves divine, this so pale death may pass you by.

Creature of the night disguised as from the sun, shall try to make humanity undone.

If one is to avoid the gaping maw, then remove the source of its song.

This is, of course, the translated version. Its original, which most people, not knowing Latin, would pass off as gibberish, is slightly clearer. Imagine the look on my face when I first read this passage: the joy, pride, sorrow, misery, dread, and many more emotions which I cannot even describe mixed into one at a single moment. After so long looking I now held the key to the great mystery that haunted every moment of my life, in these very hands it now lay open to me like a portal to another world. I really couldn't tell you how, but I knew at first glance that one little poem held all the answers that I sought. Immediately, I started studying this poem to unravel its mysteries.

"Listen and be warned of a secret of past, these warnings of a hunter to the hunted do not pass." This first part of the passage clearly stated that this was a warning of a predator from man's long lost past. Whether this creature was an ancestral descendent from a long line of fiends or had lived through all these years feeding on humans throughout the ages is not clear. One thing was clear in the warning, however; this is a creature that men, if they are unfortunate enough to meet, were not meant to survive.

The next part of the passage to me was also very clear and only took one reading to figure out its message.

"Creatures baptized by night's chrisom sheet, pray for your soul that eyes do not meet." This creature, whatever it was, had to be born of darkness and quite possibly nocturnal in nature.

"The shrieking neigh of a foe of old, shall not bode well for it has been foretold. When pale death gallops by, a mortal's time is always nigh." The shrieking neigh, an odd thing to put into a poem, don't you think? Also look at the next part of the passage, pale death gallops. These were not put into the poem for mere poetic aspect, no; Kipling was describing a creature much like a horse. Clearly he was warning us about an ancient creature which destroyed those it came in contact with.

The next part of the poem, however, I was very familiar with, as my poor little Abigail's death can attest. "Hide those, whose souls are fresh, else it shall turn to lament." This creature, unicorn, whatever it may be, feeds on the young.

I will confess that not all this poem makes complete sense to me, such as "Learn the sign of the leaves divine, this so pale death may pass you by." My best guess to this portion of the poem is that it must have something to do with the clover. After all, St. Patrick used it in Ireland to explain the concept of the Trinity.

"Creature of the night disguised as from the sun, shall try to make humanity undone. If one is to avoid the gaping maw, then remove the source of its song." The source of the song is a mystery as well, but one thing is very clear from this part of the poem and Abigail's diary. This creature comes to its prey as to a friend. The fact that this creature befriended my little Abigail before it killed her is infuriating!

No longer was I in doubt of what happened that night so long ago. With this passage something in my mind clicked and I could see what this unicorn Summer had done. He found little Abigail playing in the fields, forgotten even by her own father, and then befriended her. Then when it had its fun, it killed her. This creature I will never forgive, and if I knew where it was, I would pay it back ten times the horror it did to my Abigail, mark my words! However, I know not where it is so I give you this warning: do not leave your child's side, keep watch for these creatures who hunt them so maliciously. Do not let the message of this story be lost, but tell others my gloomy tale so they do not suffer the same fate.

- CHAPTER TWO -

THE SECRET LIBRARY

The poor beggar in the bar just stared, dumbfounded, as Jack completed his odd tale. Not sure what to think, the beggar looked down at his drink resting on top of the dirty wooden table, wondering how many of them he had and if it was enough to explain the poorly dressed, large man in front of him. The two men looked very similar, for they both wore dirty old duster trench coats and had scraggly beards which matched their long unwashed hair. Even their drinks were the same in the large dirty glass mugs which they gripped tightly with fingerless gloves. The only significant difference between the two men was their physical appearances in which Jack was obviously well built and exercised his physique.

The beggar looked around at the surprisingly empty bar for a Friday evening, as if searching for some form of escape from this crazy unicorn man. He was about to suggest to Jack that he may have had too much to drink, but at that moment Jack called for "two more drinks for me and my buddy here, on me." After that, all thought of that conversation disappeared in the beggar's mind. After all, it wasn't his place to deny such a decent person the satisfaction of getting away and forgetting, if even for a while, the unfair and cruel trick called life.

"So," the beggar began taking another gulp from his mug. "What are you going to do now?"

"Now that I found out what killed my daughter?" Jack asked. The beggar nodded in reply. "I don't know, perhaps I should search for it."

"Are you going after the unicorn then?" he asked, nearly spilling his drink as he tried not to laugh at his own question. "The one you call S...."

"Summer," Jack helped the beggar as his speech began to slow.

"Summer, I would think would be easy enough to find."

"One would think that," Jack replied, looking out the window into the moonless night sky, past a poorly lit street littered with three story buildings that were clearly unkempt, as if forgotten from the mind of their caretakers. "But this unicorn is crafty, he had to be to survive for so many years, or so the poem tells us. Our ancestors feared this creature, so I would imagine that it's a survivor and could live anywhere, maybe not even in this world."

"So it's like some kind of alien or something?" the beggar asked, for in spite of himself, he had taken interest in the man's story.

"Maybe," Jack replied, pondering this thought, "but

I doubt it. I think that it came from this world, but wherever it has come from, one thing is quite certain; it is extremely dangerous."

The beggar threw back his head, smiling to himself, thinking it silly that a unicorn could bring such fear into this large man's life. It was absurd to say the least. For this man, the beggar, still thought of unicorns as colorful happy creatures from children's stories rather than the vicious predators Jack described. "I don't see why you're so worried about such creatures existing," he finally replied. "Surely they are no real danger. After all, people sometimes die from animal attacks, but we don't fear every bird or lizard upon this Earth. In fact, if the government ever found one it would become an endangered species and protected."

With this comment, Jack's voice went lower and became wilder than before. "Do you still not understand after the story I just told you? You of the simple mind! This creature is not natural to this world! The poem clearly stated that it is a hideous, loathsome being that man was never designed to interact with. This creature is nothing more than evil and it is good if it is completely wiped from the face of the planet." Jack leaned into the table, forcing the poor startled beggar to withdraw from the now enraged man in front of him. "The creature must die; no other destiny lies before it for killing my little Abigail. He must pay the price, a life for a life as the good book would say."

"I'm not so sure the Bible says that…" the beggar began but was cut off.

"It may not say that exactly, but I am sure that destroying things of evil is in there somewhere," Jack replied, leaning back as his voice grew softer. "Just wish that I knew more about the creature."

"Maybe the last part of the poem holds your answers," the beggar said, knowing that even if they didn't, that Jack would probably find the answers anyway, like some sort of self-fulfilling prophecy.

"Yes! For they must!" Jack answered back. "But how do I find these answers? Where do I look? The library and internet yielded all that they could for me."

"Have you tried the bathroom stalls?" the beggar joked, but was taken aback when Jack answered yes. He shook his head at the reply. "This story is just too much, you know that? It borderlines crazy."

"You still don't believe?" Jack asked, crossing his arms, feeling let down by the beggar in front of him, "Even after all I have told you?"

"Of course I don't! A unicorn, I mean come on! No sane person would believe in such a thing!" Becoming instantly aware again of the person's size in front of him, the beggar immediately decided to soften the blow that he had dealt. "Of course, I never had anything happen to me such as what happened to you."

"No, I understand. It is an extraordinary tale after all," Jack replied. "To tell you the truth, if I didn't see it with my own eyes, I would surely be as the same mind as you."

"I'm sure that you saw something, but it couldn't have been a unicorn; they don't exist." The beggar took the last gulp of his beverage. "Listen, I was once a conspiracy theorist myself and I know that you think unicorns might be real, but they are not. I would believe that churches are against rock bands because they have stocks in pipe organs more than this story."

Jack slowly nodded, now losing interest in what the beggar was saying, but something that was said caught his ear. "Churches," he softly repeated to himself. "Of course!" he cried standing up. "The church! How could I have been so blind? Jonathan Kipling, the poem's author, was a devoted Catholic! He must have told them of his findings, for what better organization to warn about the unicorn, than one that fights evil on a daily basis?" He took the beggar's hand and shook it. "Thank you, my good sir! I will fol-low your advice right away." Jack spun around and left the shabby little bar, walking briskly away as his trench coat flailed behind him trying to keep up. He headed with the speed and purpose of a man on a mission as he followed a lonely cobble stone road into the night's light mist.

The beggar watched him walk into the darkness, before returning to the drink Jack had ordered earlier. The conversation had to have been one of the more interesting ones he had had for a long time. He grabbed the mug but before it reached his lips he managed to mumble out two words, "Bloody lunatic."

Jack knew that a new church would not have what

he needed to learn as he came upon his apartment door. The search had to be started at the beginning, the very church that Jonathan Kipling was a member of. As he entered his dank little room, he went straight to his book and opened it. The page he needed had long ago been creased from his careful studies of it and now the book naturally flung open to the page. His dirty finger quickly scrolled down the author's biography in which there was very little to be known about the author but what little was written held what he was looking for. Jonathan Kipling, who in 1446 died at age 47 from a plague it would seem, was a Welsh man who lived in Southern Ireland near the modern day city of Dublin.

His eyes narrowed as the realization that his search would take him out of country began to take hold. After a period of thinking the problem over and calculating what would be needed for such a trip, he sat down on his old wooden chair, head in hands. He took a deep breath as nervousness set into his mind. If he decided to tread the path before him there would be no turning back. If this creature really didn't exist, then he would be dooming himself to a pointless search. He looked around his shabby little apartment. Were things any better for him if he stayed? His life had already seemed to be heading for a dead end. Why not try a different road? After all, he had always wanted to visit Europe.

With that thought, he left the apartment, and after a short stop at the storage unit to grab his aging passport, he began making preparations for his journey. Not wanting to take the risk of his rent running out before he could make it back he paid for the future use of the storage unit in which the manager was more than willing to oblige his request.

   With everything now in order, he was ready to leave the country he knew for so long and step out into the great unknown. The day that he left, he gave his farewell grunts to his neighbors who somehow knew that he was leaving them and grunted back with more lax voices which seemed to say "Farewell, good luck, and go west young one" which of course one could call crazy that this was what these grunts meant. After all Ireland is in the East not the West. These grunters even permitted him to use the restroom before them, this was besides the fact that Jack had to wake up earlier than usual to catch his flight.

   The flight to Ireland was itself uneventful; the wait in the lounge area for the plane was long, and the conversations of the tired business folk around him stagnant, just as they were when he finally boarded the plane. He soon arrived in New York to board the second and last flight of his trip. There, he waited a few more uneventful, lazy, dismal hours before finally boarding the large aircraft destined for Dublin. Jack wasn't particularly fond of flying, for in the past it had been known to cause his usually strong stomach to feel uneasy and forced the liberation of many a past meal. He sat thankfully in the aisle of the plane. Being a large man, his seating with the aisle on one side and a skinny accountant on the other was quite comfortable. Not so for the accountant, however; this unfortunate soul happened to be sitting between two large men: Jack, who was large and muscular, and another who was not large due to extensive exercising of his physique, but quite the opposite. Both men, to the accountant's horror, radiated strong odors which clashed in ferocious battles for supremacy around him.

This odor, however, Jack did not notice as the trip unfolded; such was his concentration on his mission. He hardly paid attention as the accountant left his seat every few minutes to escape to the liberation of the bathroom from this pungent smell. He just mechanically got up letting him pass, not even fully knowing that he did so as he was preoccupied with thoughts of finding Jonathan Kipling's old church. He didn't even notice when the plane hit strong turbulence in the early hours of morning. If he did, he would have saw the wings of the airplane through the small oval windows of the plane dance in the wind as they bounced and bent in such ways that they should have snapped sending them all plummeting to the vast ocean underneath. The wisdom in their design however kept them strong even in such furious winds.

The arrival to Ireland took place just hours after the sun crept over the horizon making the ocean underneath glisten like a precious jewel. Jack had never realized it before but as he looked he could make out a slight bending upon the ocean's surface and in the immense wall of clouds before them. It was as if he could see the curve that gave the Earth her very shape. He was still contemplating this when the plane made a slight turn giving his window a sudden view of Ireland. Oh, Ireland! The first thing that anybody would notice about the land, even from such a height, is how green it really is. The land was clearly divided up much like a large checkerboard, with green grass squares separated by even greener rows of trees and bushes. There was hardly any space which was not a dark green, a healthy wonderful green which was truly a testament to the country's rich soil.

As the plane landed and the word to disembark was given, Jack was almost knocked over by the accountant who left the plane with great speed. Jack thought the little man must have been late to something very important by how he tore through the large mass of people to be the first one off the plane. Jack followed the accountant's example, although with his stomach somewhat upset from the flight he did not have the same great speed. He soon found himself at a white teller booth where his passport was checked by a particularly unhappy fellow who asked him what his business in Ireland was to be. Jack had never heard a true Irish accent before but this man had one, there was no mistaking it. The man's voice was laced with the richness and beauty of Irish speech which was the best type of welcome that Jack could think of as he entered the ancient land.

The man asked again what Jack's purpose was in Ireland, a question that he had not even thought about how to answer. Surely he could not tell this young man that he was here to search for information about a dark creature that murdered his beloved daughter. Nor, could he say that he was there to search for a church that may be part of a person's home or on their land. Either answer, although they were true, would not prove wise for one who is trying to enter another country to say. So like most American tourists, he answered that he was there to see the splendors that the country holds and learn more about his own Irish ancestry.

This answer seemed to be acceptable to the man in the booth, for he took Jack's passport and after a short check, he mechanically and unemotionally stamped it and welcomed Jack to Ireland. Jack left the man and passed many colorful gift shops where eager travelers were busy paying for overpriced knickknacks to take home to their loved ones. He quickly exited to the clean crisp unpolluted air outside. Jack could not have gotten out of the crowded building soon enough, seeing the people busy buying gifts for their family and loved ones was unbearable. It was just a grim reminder of how alone in the world he really was and why he was here.

Walking away upon the faded red cobblestone roads, he began to see the many wonders that were in Dublin. The houses in the area were simple enough, one or two stories tall with jagged multi-layer shingles that framed the chimneys which jetted out the roofs middle instead of the sides. Their faces had no plastic siding, but instead their designers seemed to have preferred a rough concrete exterior resting upon a red brick base. That's not to say that all the houses looked like these; no, there were also surfaces made of wood, strong stones, dull stones, expensive stones, cheap stones, rough stones, and stones so smooth that even a fly couldn't grip onto them to rest from its weary travels.

Most of the houses though seemed to favor brick, giving the land a very classic natural feel and look. Only a few homes were modernized in the sense of using plastics in their makeup. Upon some of these classy homes, though, there was a strange feature that anyone would find hard to miss. For upon these old homes and apartments, which were red and dark in nature, were in thick white frames many brightly colored doors, which didn't match the buildings at all or have any purpose. There were yellow doors, pink doors, blue doors, and red doors, bright neon green doors which hurt the eye to look at, and even some rich, majestic purple doors, but no black. Not once traveling down the roads was there a black door to be seen.

This mystery, though, is for another time, for if we were sidetracked into the history and rich culture of the Irish people and the struggles they had to endure, which could be seen in the many political flyers that covered every lamp post down the streets, this tale would never be finished. That said, Jack, who had traveled some distance from the airport, found himself staring at a brick domed building. The building's name was in bold Gaelic letters, but thankfully for Jack's sake there was an English translation that plainly read "library." Jack pressed open the heavy oak doors and stepped onto its polished floor, stopping a moment to study the floor's symbols of swans, fish, men toiling in hard labor, and ships sailing into fiery sunsets upon the ocean's shimmering surface. There were plants and trees of all varieties encircling the Irish harp, the very symbol of Ireland. This harp was by far one of the oldest of musical instruments that he had heard of and was on a number of the stone monuments on the city's streets.

Dublin, though did not feel like an average city. None of the buildings seemed to belong to a city; they felt too modest and warm. At least compared to the typical skyscraper laden cities in America where the buildings seem to look down, appalled at the people hurrying to keep their busy schedules. While in their cold steel heads they comfort the more powerful people in the society, which seem, like their buildings, to have the same outlook upon the poor people on the streets below, their legal prey.

However, Dublin looked to be different in every aspect. There were no overwhelming skyscrapers to magnify the everyday perception of people's insignificance. No large names on their sides to proclaim the wealth and grandness of a proud individual's status compared to the everyday citizen. One must wonder if these proud people of wealth, who think only in terms of money and class, have altogether forgotten that they are of the same mortal blood as those less fortunate whom they entertain themselves with manipulating and abusing in their particular sports.

The buildings in Dublin had none of this, even the

tallest building could only boast of a few stories. Some of
the buildings were even covered by large vines to dress
the simple structures that the Irish made, which in their
simplicity could outshine any decoration that a wealthy
man could buy. Nowhere were there smokestacks or other
pollutants to blot out the sky; the land was simple in nature
and its people touched with a Christian spirit that made it
all the more impressive compared to the large cities of this
world.

"May I help you?" a middle-aged woman asked
Jack behind her wooden desk while looking upon him
through her oval glasses.

"I was wondering if I might find some information
on a certain individual who used to live here," Jack replied. The woman stared at Jack questionably for not many
Americans come to Ireland to spend time in a library. Jack,
realizing this and not wanting to raise suspicion that would
force him to answer many an embarrassing question, added,
"I think that he may be an ancestor of mine."

The librarian nodded at his comment, believing
the lie. She lowered her guard and directed him to an old,
small, and secluded section of the library. This part of the
library looked ancient. Like a room from long ago forgotten
by time, it was filled with many worn wooden desks with
the holes cut out of them for bottles of ink to rest in. These
desks held stacks of books and fat computer monitors. The
librarian picked a book off one of these wooden desks and
placed it upon one of the hundreds of wooden bookshelves

which spewed dust upon them in gratitude of her returning its lost piece.

This part of the library was clearly hardly ever used and its books had not known the warmth of a human's hand for many a decade. Strange it must have been for them as they stared at Jack with blank quiet expressions as if they have forgotten their original purpose in the long years they slept on the shelves. To sit there as if relearning their particular function as they watched Jack open up their brothers and read the words that had been hidden in their bindings for so long. It didn't take long for that section of the library to come alive with dust as Jack skillfully pulled them out one by one and scoured their pages for any clue about Jonathan Kipling.

The librarian, to say the least, kept a sharp eye on him as she pretended to be busy in the room organizing the shelves. When she did leave the room, though, it was not for long so adamant was she on making sure that Jack knew he was not alone. Whether it was because he was foreign and out of place or the homeless look about him, she didn't completely trust Jack to be alone unsupervised in her library.

Jack soon found what he was looking for as he beheld Jonathan Kipling's information in the genealogy books and soon after checked the land records from that time. After extensive research that took a good part of the day to complete he had a good idea of where to look for the church. Surprisingly enough, the church, which was burned down long ago, was close to Jonathan's land where a distant relative of his, Mort Kipling still lived.

Satisfied with his findings, Jack slammed the book close, startling the little librarian who now stared sharply at him with her cold, calculating eyes. Eyes that would make any man sorry in an instant if they looked his way and Jack was no exception as he apologized for his rudeness and eagerly got up, making his way out of the library. The librarian stared after him disapprovingly before she took a swig of coffee as if Jack left a bad taste in her mouth. In truth, he did, for even though he was now gone, the odor that was around him still lingered in the library as she began to clean up the mess of open books that Jack left in his wake.

Jack left the library, once again traveling the streets of Dublin where he found himself in the busy tourist area just outside a very green park which fittingly enough, people called The Green. As he traveled down the busy street he could see men juggling fire on unicycles, fighting with umbrellas in skillful shows of swordsmanship, and playing musical instruments of every kind. From the classic fiddle to the electric guitar, the music could all be heard clashing in the loud crowds, clamoring for people's attention.

Everywhere he looked, there were street performers doing complicated tricks such as fitting their bodies into a tiny box, to simple tricks such as making bubbles with wands which flew above the eager and excited crowd's heads in a wobbly fashion. To the sides of the street were the performers who stood like statues, some of whom were painted to fit this look so well that the only way to tell they were real was by the open case in front of them for impressed spectators to fill with change. Of course, some of the unofficial street performers who were masters at the art of begging were also there. By sheer practice of this ancient art of liberating coinage from those around them, all but the best actors in Hollywood would be put to shame. Masters of manipulation would get close to a person's face well past their comfort zone as the victims ate at tables enjoying a nice meal, and tell of starvation and no money. Then out of discomfort and want for the clever beggar to leave, the person would give more than enough to feed the beggar, only to watch dumbfounded as the same beggar gave the same act to a table next to them. Some would try to sell old magazines, while others outright just asked for money, with no story to fill the reason for why it was needed.

As Jack moved away from the tourist areas, catching a city train, then a bus to the country side, these beggars' ranks thinned, and then disappeared entirely. The land outside the city of Dublin is like nothing that could be experienced in America, and if there is such a place that can match its deep green shaggy grass and the clean air of this untainted well-loved land, then name it! I should like to know and go there to experience all that the land will offer. Until then, when such a place is found, permit me to say again that the Irish land has been truly blessed with natural beauty which remains un-trampled and un-mangled by the inhabitants. The bus dropped Jack off at a small road before leaving him to soak in Ireland's famous changing weather. It took Jack a full three hours and three rainstorms to find Mort Kipling's house. When Jack arrived he immediately started to search the property not caring that he was completely soaked from the previous storms.

Mort, who was also a man of tall stature and strong from his work in the rocky soil, saw Jack snooping around his land. What Jack was looking for, though, neither one of them really knew for certain and after a curious thought Mort decided to find out.

"Good afternoon," Mort called to Jack, who turned to face him. "Lovely day, isn't it?"

"Yes, I suppose it is." Although Jack did not feel like it after getting soaked one minute only to have the sky clear up the next. Somewhere in heaven he felt there must be someone having fun at his expense in this matter.

Realizing that Jack was a foreigner, Mort made the conclusion that he was a lost tourist. "I don't want to be rude, but what are you doing?"

Jack thought about what to say to this man. Surely the truth of his being there would not suffice. After a quick thought, he came to the same conclusion that he had in the library, to lie. "I am from America and wanted to see the land that my ancestors came from."

"The States? How long have you been here?"

"Just today I spent most of it in the library. I wanted to find Jonathan Kipling's place before anything else."

Mort, suddenly becoming aware that Jack was

looking for his place, became very cautious of this man who he now knew was not the lost tourist that he thought at first. "Why were you looking for his place?"

"I believe that he might be a relative of mine." Jack's training and experience from being a lawyer quickly came back to him as he felt Mort's mood change to curious excitement. Now realizing that he said this to none other than the owner of the land, he had to fight his urge to smack himself on the head for his sheer stupidity. Jack's best hope was that Mort did not know much about his ancestors; then maybe, just maybe, he could get away with the lie.

Any hope of Mort being ignorant of his family history faded when Mort replied, "That must be the Klipher side; they went to America in 1846."

"That would be them" Jack spoke through his grinding teeth. He never liked being powerless in any situation and now he was in a foreign nation, snooping on someone's farm, and lying to a knowledgeable person about a family line which he had no knowledge about. As one may expect, he knew there was no chance of getting away with the lie. However, he also realized that this was his best chance to find the information that he sought, so before he was found out he would learn everything he could.

"I'm Mort, by the way, Mort Kipling," Mort said extending out his hand. "I'm a direct descendent of Jonathan Kipling, I am."

Jack returned Mort's gesture and shook hands. "I'm Jack, Jack Tanner."

"Well, Jack, come to the house, and I will have the old lady brew some tea; then we can figure out more about your lineage, shall we?"

Knowing that this was his best opportunity, Jack followed him up to a small house on the side of the hill. Grazing on the other side of a wire fence was a small herd of fat sheep which would occasionally look up at them curiously before focusing once again on the grass which beckoned to them. "This is a nice place," Jack replied.

"Much thanks," Mort replied, swelling up with pride. "This land has been in our family for over seven centuries. Many a battle was fought upon this land, but always our family kept it. Even through the Great Famine when many left, we remained. This land is in our blood and in yours. Ah, Martha," Mort stated as the front door opened to reveal a strong, fair lady with thick red hair, dark eyes, and imposing figure which Mort would tell you matched her stubborn will. Martha had the same distrusting look as the librarian which seemed to be a standard feature of the Irish women when they saw Jack.

"Who is this?" she harshly asked, squinting her eyes towards Jack, who seemed to have forgotten all together how to speak under her piercing gaze and menacing scowl. All Jack could do was sheepishly grin in return.

"This good lad is Jack; he came all the way from The States to see us. He says to be a relative of ours from the Klipher side." Martha rolled her eyes at Mort, not caring at all for his hobby of genealogy. "I invited him in for some tea."

Martha, knowing full well that her husband was a kind, good-hearted man, who once set on an idea would not budge from it, gave a disgruntled huff and opened the door for the two men to come inside. "Wipe your boots! This isn't some kind of barn you know."

"You will have to forgive my wife, she's not used to strangers."

"At least not ones that look like they came off of the streets," Martha replied.

Mort ignored her as he led Jack into the cozy five-room wood-floor home. The simple house could be described as ordinary. In the living room were a television and a couch, in the kitchen were the stove and cabinets while the dining room had a small table with a vase and flowers decorating its center. The last room that Mort showed him was his office. Unlike all the other rooms, this one was furnished with all types of books that filled shelves on all four walls. There was a small desk in the corner of the room and three cloth chairs around a thick wood table.

"Now," Mort said to himself as he searched the books, "let's see if we can figure out how you're related, friend."

Jack decided to act fast and began to pry Mort with his questions. "I understand that Jonathan Kipling's old church used to be here next to the property. Very convenient if you ask me."

"It should be; he was the one who started it," Mort

replied, still busy looking for the book.

"Started it?"

"Yes, his house used to be where the members would meet before the church was built just a little way over there," he replied, motioning to an area outside the window. "That and the fact that he was a writer is what he is best known for."

"So I have read. It's a shame that he died before he could write more works."

"That it is, but we all have to go sometime, now, don't we?"

"Yes, I suppose so," Jack thoughtfully replied. "But the plague is not what I would choose."

"Plague?" Mort asked, looking at Jack curiously.

"Yes, a book that I read said that he died of the plague. A horrible nasty death it must have been."

"I suppose it would be, but he didn't die of that. No, he was poisoned by something the physicians didn't under-stand at the time."

"How was he poisoned?"

"Well, I think that it was more an allergic reaction than poison from the stories that were told to me. Nothing too exciting to tell about." Mort reached up and grabbed another book. "Ah, here we go."

Jack looked out the window towards the setting sun. "An allergic reaction?"

"Yep, something he ate perhaps. Here we are: the Klipher side." Jack waited anxiously as Mort searched the pages. After a long while he looked up with a slight scowl on his face.

"What is it?" Jack asked, fearing the answer that would come.

"I'm afraid," Mort replied, slamming his book shut, "that this book does not have any information about the Klipher family after they left Ireland and made it to New York."

"That's a shame," said Jack as a wave of relief washed over him.

"No matter, I will have to look it up in the morning, I will. Should you like to stay for supper? Martha is a fine cook and it will do good to have some company, I'm sure."

"Not for the one cooking," Martha replied coming into the room.

Jack shook his head apologetically. "I do not wish to impose. Besides, night's coming on and I still have to find a place to stay."

"Stay with us," Mort quickly replied. "We have an extra room in the back since our son went off to college."

"Mort!" Martha hissed through her teeth.

"He has nowhere to go and we have an extra room."

"He's a stranger, Mort, and I will not have him staying in this house. He could be crazy for all we know." Mort grinned apologetically towards Jack for his wife's comments, but Martha was not sorry. She had concerns about Jack staying with them and by golly they were going to hear them. "A perfect stranger dressed like he came from the street gutters and smells like it too, staying in our house! We shall be robbed for sure. I sure hope that what he takes is mostly yours, it would serve you right."

"Listen, I can find a place in town," Jack began, but was cut off by Mort who didn't seem to hear him.

"Honey, we should be compassionate towards those who need our help."

"Why?" Martha challenged him.

"Because the Lord takes care of those who take care of others, he does."

Martha, not having anything else to combat her stubborn husband with and seeing that he was dead set on the idea gave in. "Fine! But if he is not right, it's on your head." She turned to Jack, giving him a hard look. "We have a shed out back; you can stay in there."

"Honey," Mort began, but was cut off by her piercing eyes that seemed to sternly warn against him saying anything further.

"Now, so you do not stink up the whole house," she began in a stern manner which only a mother could do, "there's a shower at the end of the hall. Get to it."

God bless that Irish woman who, not caring to spare Jack's feelings, in that one command forced him to take not only a much needed shower, but also to wash his old dirty clothes. When all that was done Jack had supper and went to the old metal shed where Mort set up a cot for him.

"I have to apologize for my wife. She's just not used to strangers coming to the house," Mort told Jack as he showed him how to work the shed's door.

"Don't worry about it; she's right, after all," Jack replied, understanding. "I wouldn't want some stranger staying in my house, either."

"Oh, where do you live?" Mort asked. "I know you're from America but what state?"

"Illinois," Jack said. "I used to have a house in the country with my wife and daughter."

"Where are they?" Mort asked, although he wasn't sure if that was a question he should be asking.

Jack's mood changed as he remembered the sorrow that he left behind. "Dead," he replied sadly.

"I'm sorry," said Mort, and he was. "How did it happen?"

Jack looked up at the night sky, fighting with himself to either remember his family and their deaths or forget them all together. Jack looked back at Mort who was patiently waiting for an answer. "My wife was taken by cancer and my daughter by a sickness, a dark and horrid sickness."

The two men stood there for a short while, not saying anything else. Mort was the one to finally break the silence. "I am sorry to hear that, Jack, I truly am. If I can do anything for you, please, let me know." Jack nodded his head as he sat down on the cot. Mort took one last look at the man and the pain that he could now clearly see him struggling with, then he quietly and respectfully shut the shed door.

After a while, Jack's dark thoughts faded into sleep, only to be woken by the baaing of sheep who while he was asleep were drawn in towards the shed by his pronounced snores. He opened the door and looked out at the softly lit night. "This is my chance," he said to himself looking up towards Mort's dark house. He had already looked around Mort's land and even the house and found no clues about Summer which left one other place: the old church. Slowly and stealthily, he made his way with a flashlight to where Mort said the church was. It took a while to find the stone rubble, which was all that remained of the old church. Over the years it had been so covered with moss and vines that it now seemed to be part of the land. It's always amazing that no matter how much man beats and burns Mother Earth, she, with gentle patience always reclaims what is rightfully hers. This stone church was by no means an exception to this amazing feat.

There was no roof, only slick mossy stone, for anything of wood disappeared long ago. Its stone pillars, that were mostly cracked and lying scattered upon the green leafy ground, were covered with so much ivy that it was impossible to pry them from the ground without the use of a knife. The only wall remaining was the back of the church, where the altar would have been. From the shape of the half oval hole in it, a majestic window must have been there as well. However impressive this building was dressed in nature's gown, it was even more impres-sive in the day, as the sun shone with full brightness upon the structure. As the day went on, Jack continued to search the old church, but he saw no clues of anything remotely related to the forces of darkness.

Jack sat on a stone pillar and gazed at the ruin which reminded him so much of himself. Oh, what a fool, he thought of himself now, a horrible wretched fool. A fool who coped with his family's death through wild searches for mythical creatures. Just another sad worthless page in his life, which like all others, ended in failure and despair. As Jack sat there crying, he thought of all he did wrong and how he failed in so many ways. First he failed his family, and then he failed himself. This thought crept into his mind and drove him to anger as he struck the stone pillar, slicing his hand on it, he let the blood it produced fall to the ground. "On this spot I swear to be better. As surely as my blood drips upon this holy ground which opens its mouth to receive it, I will do better, be better." He turned to the wall of the church. "This I promise," he swore and started back to Dublin.

He was not going to go back to Mort's, for there was no need. He found the answer that he was looking for by not finding anything. What he had thought was wrong. Summer was a creature made up by his daughter who was hallucinating from a sickness. He never saw a unicorn his eyes were playing tricks on him, and Jonathan Kipling's poem was that, just a poem. This sudden realization seemed to clear the fog from his head as he started to look at things in a clearer and brighter way. In fact it was as if a huge burden was lifted from his shoulders. This realization even made him laugh. Contrary to that old belief that a failed mission would bring misery to the person, for Jack it was quite the opposite. He now looked back at everything that he had done and realized just how silly it was.

It would have been a wonder to anyone who would have seen such a sudden change in a person's attitude. In fact, if they had not known the story of Jack's life, it would have been alarming. But there he was, making his way through the brush humming to himself, not caring anymore of dark shadows or bumps in the night. His mission hit a dead end. He could finally go on with his life. This knowledge brought a flood of emotions of relief and joy which the sacred ground of the good little church had been a stranger to for many ages. The loss of his family still tore at his heart, and it always would, but at last there seemed to be a ray of sunlight in this dark, dank world.

It was perhaps the fact that he was not looking where he was going, or divine intervention which had some other plan for him, that as he made his way through a particular dense brush pile he racked his shin against an ancient grave stone, part of an overgrown and forgotten cemetery next to the church. Of course he looked down to read the stone that he struck, needing to know who to curse for being inconsiderate enough to have placed his tombstone where he was walking.

However, as he read the name, he dropped to his knees. "No, no, you accursed stone!" he cried. "You wicked stone! Years of happiness would I have had if you had not shown your ugly face to me, destroyer of lives and fouled with rotten flesh! Oh, how I loathe you and all you represent, you who are cursed even by those cursed. May the sun never shine brightly upon your face again and you crumble in silent solitude with no one to take care of you or even weep for you as the Day of Judgment slowly approaches you and your master. May not a day go by that is not filled with sorrow for penance of the wrong you have done me, you who are cursed and damned beyond all others in this world." Jack took a fistful of dirt and smeared it upon the stones words. "I blot you from my vision but cannot do so from my mind. The harm that was done shall stay with me forever, so I curse and spit at you, Satan's tool most foul."

Jack angrily got up and headed back towards Mort's residence. Yes, Mort's, as you may have already guessed, that tombstone was Jonathan Kipling's, and just like what one could expect from a famous poet, he left one final clue on the stone before his passing. The words destroyed Jack's short-lived hope of a normal life.

Upon my land the hills of old, there is a place that a story is told.
The fight of a mortal and a horned fiend never did go unseen.
Go into the sinking sun, dip your head in and cool your tongue.
Down into the cracked wall, is where you shall find this
infamous song.

Jack quickly made his way back, for he knew

exactly what he was looking for. When he stared out of
Mort's study's window the other day he had glanced at a
pond that touched the side of a hill. There he saw the red
sun seem to dip into the pond's glossy surface. It was not
the real sun, of course, just its reflection, but there was no
other explanation that could be drawn from the poem. The
day was clear for thankfully the sky's other, wetter personalities, which it seemed to play fondly with in this part of
the world, were quiet, and showed proudly in its sky the
sun which luckily had just begun to set. Soon Jack made it
to the farm. Looking towards the pond, he saw it, the sun
red in color reflecting on the pond's surface seeming to dip
itself into this secluded bath.

Jack went to it, how could he not? The poem had
led him to this place, and if he left without at least taking a
look he would surely regret it for the rest of his life. Even
if he returned to America and started a new life, which he
had sworn to do before the gravestone so rudely disturbed
his plans, he would regret it. Jack's consolation though was
that the farm was so close and if this last clue did not yield
results, he could move on with a lighter heart. Jack soon
came to the pond's edge and after a moment's hesitation he
stripped down to his briefs then plunged himself into the
water. Along the rocky hill's wall, he felt with his hands as
the curious sheep looked on, wondering with not much wisdom, what he was doing and if it affected them. They soon
lost interest and went back to their grazing before night
came and called them to sleep. If only I were one of those

sheep and life was so simple!

Jack searched the cliff, but to his secret joy, there was no crack in its hard rock surface. Just as he decided to leave the pond and start his life anew, a sudden thought gripped his mind and he began to search the wall under the water's surface. His hope quickly faded as the cliff turned out to overhang an enormous horizontal crack that he could easily squeeze through. With a curse on his tongue, Jack took a deep breath and dove under the overhang, groping his way blindly along the crack. It didn't take him long to reach the other end where to his amazement was a huge pocket of air, more like a cave than anything else. As he stepped upon dry stone, he turned on the flashlight to see a thick wooden door at an end of a long manmade shaft filled with rotten barrels. Losing all hope of escaping his fate, Jack moved somberly towards the door.

As he opened it, such an array of books could be seen in polished wooden shelves that it was a wonder how so many could fit inside of this little manmade cavern in the hill. On the walls were old burnt torches held on with rusty metal braces overlooking a small table with a book already opened on it, as if signaling him to read it. The book was not about a unicorn but instead was about a line of Catholic members that used to live in the area. Jack did not realize it at the time, but most of the works in the library were Catholic, hidden away from the group's enemies. This knowledge, however, Jack would learn later, for as he looked upon the shelves his eye caught sight of a nice, well-bound book on Catholic history. The book looked strange, almost new compared to the other books on the shelf. Curious, he began to read some of its content. Imagine his surprise when he realized that this book was recently published. Imagine more of his surprise when at the moment of re-alization of this that the lights in the cave were turned on, casting away the shadows of the dark, revealing him and the entirety of the room.

- CHAPTER THREE -

A BATTLE AGAINST THE DARK

There Mort stood with books in hand, staring in utter amazement at the shirtless man standing in the middle of his family's most hidden place. Jack also stared at Mort not knowing what to say or even if he could say anything to the man to explain what he was doing. Both of them looked at each other, not unlike a deer to a car's headlights before the clash of flesh and metal. Mort was the first to speak. He did so cautiously, not knowing how or why Jack broke into his family's hidden library.

"What are you doing here?" he asked. Jack gently put the book back on the shelf and took a step closer to Mort. "No, I think that you should stay there for the time being."

"Fair enough," Jack replied, noticing how tense Mort had become. "I am sorry; if I had known that you knew about this place I would have asked before I came in."

"Didn't know! The door is in the basement! How much more obvious could it have been?" Mort replied harshly, and understandably so.

"You're kidding me," Jack replied. "All that work and the door to this place was in plain sight all along?"

"What are you talking about, plain sight?" Mort replied. "The doors under the rug and a chair." he then thought about what he just said. Remembering that he had just removed the two items off of the door just a minute ago before entering the cave through a skinny tunnel he exclaimed. "The door was still covered, you couldn't have used it! How did you get in here?"

"Under the cliff in the pond there's an entrance; the one that Jonathan Kipling's last poem told about. It lead me here."

"He wrote no such poem," replied Mort. "I have every one of his books and never once did he describe such a thing."

"It was on his tombstone next to the old church," Jack answered bitterly remembering the foul poem that crushed his short lived dream of a normal life.

Mort raised an eyebrow in slight confusion at Jack's reply, but he soon regained his composure. "Oh, by the way, I found something interesting that you should know," Mort replied, taking a dagger off of a small table that he had slowly been working towards. Now with the cold steel object in hand he became bolder in his speech. "I found out today that the Klipher family's line ended when they arrived in New York all those years ago. A horrible murder it was, over a measly dollar bet on a fight. Now tell me, man from America, if that is truly where you are from. Why did you come here?"

Jack, seeing himself in such a bind, frantically searched for ideas of how to handle the anxious man with the menacing knife. He thought of a dozen lies, each one more clever than the last, but a voice inside him said that they would not suffice. So at last, when the little voice that mortal men call a conscience won out, the truth was told. "Mort," Jack began, "you're right, I am not part of the Klipher family. In fact I had not even heard of them until you mentioned them yesterday."

"Why are you here?" Mort replied, gripping the knife harder.

"I am here for my daughter's sake." Mort looked at him curiously but did not say anything to this so Jack continued. "My daughter, my little Abigail, was not taken from me by a sickness or any other normal enemies of the mortal life. Her destroyer was too cruel and wicked to be counted amongst their ranks. It is a wicked creature of darkness and a curse upon mankind, one that I will hate forever."

Mort cleared his throat. "Was this creature that you speak of, you?" he asked, afraid of the answer.

At these words, Jack's heart, felt like something pierced through it. "It is true that I had a part in her sad fate, but God forbid, I never could have done such a thing!" Jack took a few steps away, remembering all that he had done wrong as a father. "Abigail deserved better than me,

I know this. I failed her! Drunken with the bottle of despair from my wife's death, I could not see what was happening. I should have stopped it!" Jack slammed his fist into a bookcase making Mort jump. "Do you know what it's like to lose a child? Do you know the horror it brings?"

"No."

"I pray you never do," Jack replied. "It's a pain beyond any other, a dark blistering pain that never ceases. It's as if a piece of your very soul is ripped away from you and a dark canyon takes its place to swallow the rest of you whole. There is no escape from this hungry void." Jack wiped his eye, holding back an ocean of tears. Through daily practice, however, he learned to hold this in check where all that could escape were a few sudden drops of salty tears and a slight tremor in the throat. "Then add this with the pain of losing a wife? It's just too much for a man to bear," he continued. "So soon, the two most important people in my life were taken away by that accursed foe of man, Death. How I wish to see its face the day the Lord comes and destroys that wicked creature and man no longer has to fear its dreadful sting! The sting of destruction and ruin!"

Jack looked at his hands which were now trembling with fear and regret. "I have only one goal now, Mort," he replied, looking up at the confused and very concerned Irish man. "I must find the creature that killed my little girl and send it back to Hell where it belongs!" His voice then became softer and more mild as if pondering a question deep in his soul, "Then maybe, just maybe, I can escape this cage of solitary despair of the past. If I confront this beast, then I may finally be rid of this rightful punishment for failing my family and move on." Jack didn't really think this would be the case, but he still hoped that somehow this journey would lead to his release from the sorrow in his heart.

Mort didn't know what to say. What Jack said pulled at his heart such was the despair in Jack's voice when he spoke. He still doubted Jack's intentions, but what he was told was the truth; there was no mistaking it. No amount of practice from any type of actor could copy the unmistakable truth that is in a person's voice laced with despair such as Jack's was now. Even though Mort may have looked menacing with knife in hand and glaring at Jack with extreme mistrust, he was not a man that could fulfill his unspoken threat. He was never one to cause another harm, even in such a situation. As long as Jack didn't do anything foolish to force him to use the knife, there was no danger. Jack had made up his mind that he would cause as little trouble as possible. After all, this was Mort's property and he was the one trespassing. The two men, unwilling to act against each other, just stood there and stared at each other not sure what would happen next.

"What now?" Jack asked.

"I'm thinking," Mort slowly replied, trying to buy time to come up with a clever solution. He had years to think about what he would do in such a situation, but until now, he never thought it possible that the library would ever be found by an outsider. Even now it was hard to believe. Unlike his grandfather who would have shot Jack on sight, Mort had no clear response for this intruder.

As they stood there looking staring at each other, something had been on Jack's mind. It was a small detail but it gnawed at him like a dog on a bone. A simple question, and one of significant proportions. Why had Mort not called the police? Jack knew from years of his practice in law that during break-ins the first thing that most homeowners did was try to reach the police. Mort had a phone. Jack saw it yesterday when he was invited into the house. It was strange to him now that Mort did not simply go back the way he had come, shut the door and bar it, and call the police. This act, or rather lack of action, was strange. Even stranger was Mort's face, which was like a man caught in some secret act. The longer that Mort stood there not knowing what to do, the more the answer was revealed until at last Jack could wrap his head around the mystery. Mort was hiding something! Something in this very room. Yes! That had to be it. Jack, breaking the awkward pause between the two men, decided to test this theory.

"This is an interesting place," Jack said, making poor Mort jump at the sudden sound of his voice. Looking around at the dusty shelves of books and noticing their age, he continued in a businesslike manner, "This library has been here for a while hasn't it?"

Mort, cautiously answered his question. "Yes," he

said putting his hand fondly on the side of a particularly old and dry bookcase, "this place has been in my family even before Jonathan Kipling's time."

"This place," Jack pressed, "it's a family secret, isn't it?"

Mort was taken aback by Jack's rightful guess but regained his composure as he thought about what to do and weighed his options. He gave a heavy sigh knowing that defeat was at hand, defeat not by wit or strength, but by the truth. So long this place had been a secret but unlike his forefathers, he could not do what was needed to be done to keep his family's deepest secret from this outsider. His only consolation was that Jack seemed to have been led here for some reason, and that it was possibly the Lord's will for Jack to learn what he needed to heal from what happened to his family. Pocketing the knife, to Jack's great relief, Mort made his way to the table, keeping a sharp eye on Jack. "Sit down," he firmly said, pointing at a chair at the old wood table. Jack obeyed, wanting to keep the knife sheathed in Mort's pocket and knowing that this was a critical moment in their conversation.

Mort took an old binder off a shelf and placed it on the table for Jack to see. He then took to a stool just beyond the table between Jack and the door. "What is this?" Jack asked, looking at the binder which contained pieces of some sort of ledger carefully preserved in plastic sleeves.

"That is the reason for this place," Mort answered. "You see, before Jonathan Kipling this place was used to hide weapons being smuggled to the warring tribes of Ireland. Many times this land was raided, and even though they found the other hidden places of my family, they never did find this place. The mere fact that this place was never found is what makes it so valuable to my family and their pride."

"But what's with all the books?" Jack asked, looking around the dry, well-lit room in appreciation and wonder.

"For safeguarding," Mort replied, looking at the bookshelves with recognition and pride before returning his gaze to Jack. "Jonathan started the collection of documents that you see in this cave and stored them here. He was afraid that they were going to be destroyed in a war or attempted purge of the Catholic faith. Of course, all of the books here were not part of Jonathan's original collection but were added afterwards. You must understand, Jack, that this place is very important to me, as it was to my ancestors. It's importance throughout the family's history and the likelihood for its future use demands secrecy."

Jack nodded his head in understanding. "I will keep your secret." He then looked at the library. "But I ask that I may use this library to find the answer that I seek about my daughter's death."

"I guess I have no choice but to believe your word on this, do I? Very well. You may use the library, but only if you are careful of the books in it. Some are very old and fragile," he replied, motioning towards a glass case filled with old books and papers that Jack had missed in his original scan of the cave.

"What's in there?" Jack asked.

"Jonathan Kipling's journal," Mort replied, carefully studying Jack's reaction to what he said. Jack, forgetting all about Mort and his knife, stood up and went towards the case. Mort immediately blocked him from the case. Not in an overly threatening way, but just enough to make Jack stop. "I cannot let you touch those documents, Jack," he said sternly. "They are very old and fragile."

"I used to be a lawyer," Jack assured him. "I know how to handle documents." Seeing that Mort was not budging, he pulled out his wallet and showed his credentials.

It was a simple gesture, but to Mort it made all the difference. Mort was now able to verify Jack's story of who he was, and as weird as it may seem, knowing that he was a lawyer, a man of law, gave him some comfort that Jack wasn't as crazy as he seemed. However, even if Jack had been the United States President himself, he was not going to risk the chance of his family's heirlooms being ruined.

"That will not do," Mort replied, going to the case. He put on white cotton gloves and slowly unsealed the glass cover. "I will handle them for you."

Jack, knowing that this was the only way that Mort would agree to let him see the journal, agreed to this condition. "That's fine," Jack said. "As long as I find out what killed my daughter I care not how the information is acquired."

Hearing these words, Mort was reminded of a

question that he had long forgotten but its importance had not diminished in his mind. Being careful not to destroy his and Jack's weak treaty, he humbly asked, "Jack, I have to know. How did your daughter die? You never did tell me."

"You're a Christian, are you not, Mort?" Jack asked after a moment of thought.

"I am," Mort said proudly.

"Then it is safe to assume that you believe in demons, is it not?" Jack continued.

"It is," Mort answered, raising an eyebrow.

"What if I told you that I believe a demon was the one responsible for my little girl's death?" Jack asked. He decided to keep the appearance of the demon he had in mind secret, not wanting to jeopardize the rare and tenuous privileges that he was recently given with Kipling's secret library. "Is this suspicion so odd to you? Even after you just admitted you believe in such creatures?" Jack asked when Mort did not reply to his explanation.

Mort never had trouble believing in the all-powerful deity and his role of good in human lives, but for some reason, the thought of demons roaming the Earth and playing the ghastly role of destroying people's lives was hard to accept. That he never gave it much thought, or the idea was too horrible to admit, he had no idea. Shouldn't he believe in the existence of demons as much as the Creator? If so, why didn't he? Then a dreadful realization came into his mind and filled him with shame. That perhaps the reason that he believed in God more was because he could see his actions and movements more clearly. This meant that either demons were sneakier in their approach, or more likely that mankind had rolled around in the pigsty of sin so much that God's works were stranger to them and stood out more than demons'. Mort, had just one other question that he needed answered and asked it solemnly, "Why did you come here?"

"Because," Jack replied, "I need your help. I want to find out what truly happened to my daughter and cannot do that unless I can unravel Jonathan Kipling's riddle. On his tombstone he wrote the fight of a mortal and a horned fiend never went unseen. I believe that he saw the very demon that I am looking for." He pointed at Jonathan Kipling's journal. "And I believe that he wrote the story in this very book."

Mort thought carefully about what Jack said. The passion and belief in his theory was undeniable, which sparked Mort's curiosity about his ancestor. Mort wanted to know more about what this man knew about Jonathan. As Jack told his belief about his daughter's death, Mort felt that something in Jack had changed. What it was he could not tell. Being true to his word, and wanting to learn more about his ancestor, Mort still decided to let Jack use the library, and it was a good thing too! Jack, who had heated himself up with the speculation of Jonathan's journal being the key to unlocking his daughter's death, had changed. He no longer cared about getting Mort's permission and was now determined to see the journal not caring anymore about the knife or even the person holding it. If Mort had denied him access to the journal then, Jack would have taken it. Thankfully though, Mort decided otherwise and this confrontation never came to pass.

Opening up the small, time-worn, black journal of Jonathan Kipling, Mort began to read of this fascinating man's life. Jonathan even from a young age did not have an easy life. He was ten when his father died of an infection from a knife wound he received in a bar fight. Ironically, that seemed to be the only night that he was not directly involved in one of these fights, according to Jonathan. After his father was killed by a knife aimed for another, Jonathan being the oldest, had to support the family of seven. He was able to keep the rocky farm, even with the massive pressure of debt that his father accumulated and left them with. If it had not been for the kind heart of a neighbor, and the occasional items that he had Jonathan smuggle for him, the people his family owed the debt to, whom Jonathan called the spawns of Satan feasting on the dreams of the helpless, would have taken their land.

Even though the stress weighed heavily on Jonathan, he kept a cheerful attitude which was strange considering he had his childhood stripped away so horribly. Jonathan's patient waiting and belief in the Lord kept him strong even through the rough trials of keeping a farm running on unfavorable land, raising his brothers and sisters after his mother passed a few years after his father, and the everyday battles with the spawns of Satan feasting on the dreams of the helpless. It wasn't until his later years that the story in the journal switched from past memories to daily written accounts. Jonathan Kipling, at this time taught himself to read and write to impress a young lady, who would later become his wife. He began to write about important matters as they happened in his life. Some of the accounts were daily and lasted for weeks, some accounts distanced by weeks. It seemed that he wrote in the journal only when he felt the need to. The handwriting became steadier as the book went deeper and became fancy. Mind you, it was not the fancy scribble that some would find on prescriptions from their local doctor, for it was still legible. His writing at first was clear and direct but as they read further it became more poetic and distinct to Jonathan's personality.

They had managed to read much of the beginning of Jonathan's life when she came in, Mort's wife. At the sight of her husband and Jack sitting at the table researching the journal, Martha gave a loud "Hmp!" making sure Mort heard her and looked. "I see that you will let anyone see this place if they show interest in that crazy family of yours."

"Dear," Mort began, getting up and carefully shutting the journal, "It isn't what you think."

"Three years you kept this place from me Mort," she said, not caring about any excuses Mort may have had to offer. "Three years I lived here, and then when I found this place while cleaning, that crazy grandfather of yours tried to shoot me!"

"Honey, you know he was sick," Mort protested. "He thought he was keeping this place a secret from outsiders."

"I was your wife!" Martha exclaimed.

Mort nodded his head, conceding her point. "I know, dear, he was wrong, but in his defense he knew that I was the only one allowed in here. He thought you were an intruder."

"Don't give me that!" she glared at him. "Three years of living with that man, taking care of him every day. He knew who I was."

"He was sick," Mort said again. "You know that."

"He was crazy even before that, God rest his soul, he was." Martha looked at Jack, slanting her eyes in disapproval. "He would have never have approved of your bringing this stranger down here."

"Actually," Mort replied, biting his lip, "I didn't let him down here, he err, kind of broke in."

Martha was flustered at this news. "Kind of broke in?" she demanded. "How did he kind of break in? How.... is he...what does he want? I should call the police!" She began moving towards the door, but her husband stopped her saying that there was no need for that.

"I am not here to rob you or harm your family in any way," Jack reassured her. "I am looking for answers and was led here; it's really quite simple when you think about it." As if the whole situation could be thought of as simple.

"You broke into our house!" she hissed with malice. There are many things in this good world of ours that I cannot claim to understand. However, the feelings of anger, fear, and mistrust in a homeowner finding an uninvited stranger in their home seems to be the norm for those unfortunate enough to find themselves in such a situation. So, to say that Martha was feeling all three of these emotions would not be hard to understand. This said, it is also easy to understand why she decided to grab the old style gun off a display case; the same one Mort's grandfather threatened her with, and point it in Jack's direction. "Get out!"

Jack, by careful observation of the gun, however, was unafraid. It was an old design which needed to be cocked first. Being cautious, knowing how quickly that could change, he replied, "No."

"He was sent here for a reason, dear," Mort quickly interjected not wanting the situation to escalate. "Once he has found what he needs, he will leave; isn't that right?" he said, turning towards Jack for confirmation.

"I will."

"See honey? There is no need for that," said Mort, motioning for her to lower the gun.

She, however, did not comply with his wishes. "Fine," said Martha after a moment of hesitation, "but I'm keeping the gun! You may trust him, but I don't." She gave a cold stare towards Jack. "Stay here with your sketchy friend, see if I care," she finished, still talking to her husband. In truth, Martha did care about Mort's safety, but for now she had to trust his judgment about Jack. Besides, if the situation got out of hand she still had the gun. The security that the old relic gave her helped her nerves, if only a little. Mort, knowing full well that his wife was comforted by this fact, decided with his better judgment not to reveal that the gun was actually empty. Even while Martha watched the two men work with a sharp eye and a cold glare that would make an eagle jealous, Mort never hinted of her threat against Jack being an empty one.

They worked throughout the night and after a quick rest at a nearby hotel, for Martha would not have him staying on the property, Jack was back in the library with Mort. But there was still no mention of any demons or creatures of darkness in the journal. They pressed on to the other works in the room. The other books did mention demons and other evil things, but none mentioned unicorns. To tell the truth, it was frustrating to Jack, who knew that he was so close, but could not find the creature he was looking for. It was even more frustrating for Mort, who did not know that they were searching for a unicorn and thought that the other books on demons should have answered Jack's questions. He and Martha discussed this at great lengths. Through their combined wisdom, they had concluded a possible but unlikely answer. However unlikely it seemed to be, their idea kept returning to Mort's mind, until one day of intense research he finally decided to get an answer. "Jack, we need to talk."

Jack, who was busy unraveling the Latin language

of an old scroll on the table, looked up. After seeing the puzzled, almost anxious expression on Mort's face, he had a feeling about what Mort was going to say. After the last few weeks they had worked together, Jack had become familiar with Mort's and Martha's personalities and could now make an educated guess of what they were thinking. "What is it?" He asked.

I want you to be honest with me, Jack," Mort said, putting down a book. "I know that there is something that you're not telling me."

"What do you mean?" Jack asked, although he already knew what Mort was going to say.

"I mean that if you were trying to find out about demons you would have found your answers by now." Mort narrowed his eyes. "You're looking for specifics on a creature," he continued, "and I'm not talking about the horned fiend description that Jonathan's tombstone mentioned." By the look on Jack's face and the sudden change in his demeanor, Mort knew that he was close to the truth. "Tell me the truth; you saw the creature, didn't you?"

Jack sat there for an uncomfortable while thinking of how and if he should answer the question. It wasn't that he was embarrassed but thought that it was too unbelievable and Mort would ask him to leave as soon as he heard the word unicorn. He looked around the old cave that seemed to hum with an old steady life, then back at its kind caretaker that stood there patiently waiting for Jack's response. He was closer than ever to his answers about

Summer. The answer was in the cave's multitude of books.
It had to be! Why should he risk losing the opportunity to
research them by telling the truth? He decided to make up
a plausible excuse, but before the words could come out a
sudden feeling washed over him. A feeling that told him
to stop lying and trust Mort. Perhaps he couldn't explain
it even if he wanted to, but Mort was the closest thing to a
friend that he had had for many years. Not only had Mort
let him use his family's secret library, but Mort was helping
with his search. Jack, for the first time, realized that he was
not alone on his journey. Whether they were sent to help or
it was by coincidence, he was grateful. Even if Martha was
always holding that gun threatening him, he was grateful.

"Jack?" Mort interrupted his thoughts.

Jack knew that he had to tell Mort the truth. It just
had to be done. He had to disclose his dark past and even
though it would be hard, he was prepared to do it. He told
cautiously his story carefully picking his words and watching Mort's face for any hint of his thoughts. He began with
his wife's passing and the despair that came after. Fighting
tears he told of his daughter's death and his discovery of
the journal, then of his long search for the creature called
Summer. To his amazement, Mort didn't react judgmen-
tally. Instead, it was a reaction of surprise followed by
deep contemplation. When Jack completed his story, Mort
said nothing but went straight to a distant bookshelf and
pulled off a slender book, worn from age and use, which he
quickly opened. Mort's worry was tangible as he brought

the book to Jack.

Jack, realizing that this was the answer he was seeking, took the book into his trembling hands. Its cover was rough and worn and showed abuse through its long life by the children that read it. It was indeed a children's book, but it was ripe with hidden meanings and messages. Its yellowed pages showed with dull brilliance on the section that Mort opened to but even though it was aged, its deep dark lettering was still very legible. Jack looked at the story that Mort had opened and read its title out loud, "A Battle Against the Dark." The sound of its title sent a shiver down his back, he knew this was the answer that he has been searching for so long.

Careful not to harm the book's fragile pages, he began to read the story inside:

Friends of God and of angels galore, the demons of past cannot be ignored.

Love ones weep and children shriek of the tale that is in store.

During a pale moon near a secluded lagoon a creature was seen. Coat of the purist white, and a horn proclaiming its might, it shone as from the sun. In the still of nights when the moon was just right its music could be faintly heard. It was soft and sweet like the birds and the bees and all would listen to its call. Children would come and meet this creature so sleek; him they came to adore. One by one, then dozens by dozens, his words poisoned their souls. The ones who came were taken and fell, with a sickness of the soul.

Then he ate and had his fill; of mortal life he had no fear, crushing families with these weekly meals. No mercy he had, and what's more than that his boldness grew with the old. Children we took and hid, then the priesthood's orders were given, and we were sent out to destroy this creature of old. Then my brother Henry and I took to the countryside with others to fight this fearsome foe.

After many an outing, groups began to vanish, later to be found completely drained of their souls. The men were great warriors indeed, and fell with a fight it seemed, which showed just how desperate our plight had become. Mortal hands and tools of iron just could not hurt this creature or shun him. Our efforts were all but for naught.

When hope was at the lowest a man from God to us showeth just how to defeat this demon and its wicked song. Careful of the leaves of three, for its power could harm even we, he spread it on our blades and bade us to be on our way, for the time of the creature's next strike was today and that night it would seem my group of three was the next in line.

Burdolf, a good friend of mine, was first to go. His muffled screams were never known, as Henry and I went forth on our way. Over logs and thickets, past sheep from the clan of Lynkets we searched for our devious foe. Then during the hours of deep sleep, at a prairie next to a stream, a soft glow in the grasses deep was seen. Knowing that it was our time, we did not turn and hide but brandished our swords towards the foe.

After a short breath, forward we slowly crept, only to stop from its chuckling song. A wave of golden mist shot up and me slightly missed, but my brother Henry I soon found was gone. Through the brush I ran, towards a soft glow in a den. There the creature over my brother was. Henry's bright soul I just saw, as it entered the creature's maw, death shrouded my brother. Its appetite still not filled, the horned stallion's gaze quickly fell towards me to be its next meal.

"Creature of the flesh, you shall be next; darkness will cloud your soul," he happily sung. "Escape there is none, your time is done. To me and we shall be whole."

Grabbing a cross, I held it up with much trust, but the creature only chuckled at my show.

"Those of the faith, in me no difference make, all shall fall to my song."

With this he charged with hunger in his eyes, ready to be quenched with my soul. My time seemed to be done and I couldn't run, so I stabbed at it with my sword. With a hiss like frying cakes it pierced the foe's mane and ran deep into its wicked side. With a twist, the sword broke, strained from its heavy yoke but its job it managed to do. With eyes of surprise, the creature slowly slipped by, and made his taunting goodbye. "Hurt I may be, but from this I will recover with ease, by then though your time will be spent. But bear this in mind, your friends shall forever be mine, failure

*is your only reward. For I am the light of the night, the ter-
rible night and I, Summer, shall always return!"*

*Now poetry cease for this tale was deep, and every
word should be learned.*

Jack was stunned. It was Summer! It was him! Here
was the proof he was looking for! In a children's book, no
less. Although by this time the idea that it was written to be
a children's book altogether flew from his mind. This was,
without a doubt, a recount of Jonathan's confrontation with
the unicorn, no doubt about it. Jonathan fought and even
managed to hurt it. He was still contemplating this when
Mort spoke up, bringing him slightly out of his thoughts.
"What do you think?" Mort asked.

He asked the question because truthfully he didn't
know what to think himself. He had never thought of the
story as anything but a children's book. But after hearing
Jack's tale he was unsure what to think. The whole situation
was frightening to the poor sheep herder.

"Henry was a brother of Jonathan's was he not?"
Jack asked, piecing the information together.

"He was."

"He died just a few weeks before Jonathan, am I
correct?"

"He did," Mort replied, remembering what was
written in Jonathan's diary. "It said that he died from the
touch of evil, but I always thought that it was a plague.
What do you think this all means?"

"I think," Jack replied, with newfound determination, "that I have finally found my answers." He turned to Mort. "The creature, Summer, that your ancestor fought has recovered from its wound and is back to prey on mankind once again."

– CHAPTER FOUR –

THE CILACK

"A unicorn?" Mort said softly, not fully able to wrap his mind around the idea of a demon being in such a form. "Why a unicorn?"

"I've pondered the same thing," Jack admitted, "but it does make sense. Evil often hides itself as things that are good to attract those around it." Jack shut the story and stared at its cover which had a faint blue image of a unicorn on it. "The devil still shows himself as a thing of good even though he is not. He does this in order to attract people to him; it's only natural that the demons that follow him will do the same." He turned to Mort who was in a state of disbelief and shock at what Jack was telling him. "It's what a lantern fish does in the dark to attract its meals. This thing, as the story told us, preys mainly on children, so it developed a form that they would be comfortable with."

Mort, who was still trying to rationalize this conversation, took a seat in one of the wooden chairs. He wasn't fully able to comprehend everything that was said but somehow in his heart he knew that it was quite right.

Many evil things that have happened in this world were disguised as good in the beginning. He looked about him at the library as if trying to find some clue as to what to do next. His eyes rested upon the diary of Jonathan Kipling. "One thing concerns me, Jack," he answered, remembering how the diary and story ended. "Jonathan's wife wrote in the last page of the diary that he died from a sickness, something described like an allergic reaction." He looked at Jack, who was listening very intently. "He died weeks after his brother." He could tell that Jack knew what he was going to say, but he was still going to say it just to make sure that he knew what could happen. "If this story about his fight with a unicorn is true, then the confrontation, the mere fact of him being in its presence, might have been the thing that killed him." Jack shifted his stance but said nothing, so Mort continued, "What I am saying is, if this story is true and you do find this creature, you will likely perish."

Jack felt a slight tremor in his stomach at these words but was unmoved from his mission. The thought had already occurred to him, but he decided to see this through until the end, whatever it was. "I do appreciate your concern," he finally replied, "but this is my mission, my purpose, and I must see it through."

"Then I suppose you are going to try to find Summer and kill him?"

"I am," Jack replied sternly.

Seeing that Jack's mind was unwavering, Mort gave a grunt of acceptance of this man's determination.

"At least now you know that it can be killed," he replied. Even though he could not fully believe that such a creature existed, he decided to help Jack find what he needed for his quest.

"That," Jack replied, "and the fact the creature according to the story hunted in the same general area." After a short pause to figure out what this meant, he continued more to himself than to Mort. "If I can find where he struck last, he will most likely be in the same area."

Mort took the book from Jack and opened it. "The first sentence that Jonathan mentioned was about the moon. Then he mentioned it again a sentence later when talking about the creature's song. I don't claim to be an expert in how my ancestor wrote, but I can tell you that he put those in for a reason, he did. The creature is somehow affected by the moon."

"Like the tides of the ocean?"

"Exactly!" Mort agreed, and then pointed to the words in the book. "It's right here! *During a pale moon near a secluded lagoon, a creature was seen.* Then again, *in the still of nights when the moon was just right, its music could be faintly heard.* The man of God In the story must have figured this out too, because he warned them that the time of the next strike was that day."

"You're right," Jack replied with a deeper appreciation of the knowledge in the book. "You think that Jonathan could have been clearer in his writings."

"That he could have," Mort agreed, "but at the time

this was probably common knowledge. After all, it sounds like the whole community was after this beast."

Jack went to a distant bookshelf and began to skim its over-packed shelves when at last he found a book of interest and pulled it out from other books' tight embrace. It was a particularly old book that he had read before but had not thought of its importance until now. Quickly he skimmed through the pages, and came to the chapter that had been on his mind. Coming back to the table, he plopped it in front of Mort to read.

It only took Mort a minute, and then he gave him a nod of agreement. The book was on St. Patrick and how he used the clover to show the people the true meaning of the trinity. "Three leaves, one stem, all separate but the same" Jack replied. "This plant must be a holy one, to be used by a saint."

"I think you are right," Mort admitted, handing the book back to him.

"I now know the creature's routine, how to look for him, and even how to kill him," Jack replied, then gave a slight grin of satisfaction. "Now all I need to do is find him."

"His routine?"

"Yes," Jack admitted, "his routine, when he takes people's souls must be the same moon as the story tells us, and the moon that he took my Abigail on was a half moon, exactly half." Jack didn't know if there was any signifi-cance to a half moon, and truth be told he didn't care as long as he could have his revenge for his beloved daughter. "That is when he showed himself to his pursuers, and that is when I will get my revenge," he said, sure of his bold statement.

"There is no guarantee of the moon having anything to do with this demon's actions," Mort commented. "It's just a theory so don't rest all your hope on it." He was still unsure of what Jack would find from this search, but he was now sure that it *would* be something after what he had seen and heard. Perhaps his wife was right and Jack was just a crazy, but he was a crazy with some credible proof. For that children's story about Summer was the only one to exist and it never left the cave or his family's lips.

They spent much of that day studying books and planning how Jack would deal with the demon if he did encounter it. Jonathan's story was a big help in this aspect. At last, Jack felt that he could really defeat Summer. Jack wanted to leave for America as soon as he learned how to kill the demon which had haunted his dreams for far too long but after Mort insisted that he stay the night, he did.

That night, Jack and Mort had supper and stayed up talking like two good friends, and in truth they were. They were not when they first met, but after so long working together to find the answers Jack sought, they had become friends. Even though Mort arranged for Jack's flight back to America, he was going to miss him. However, the same couldn't be said for Martha who was all but glad to see Jack go. If not because he broke into their home and forced himself onto their land for almost a month, then for the mere fact that she wouldn't have to prepare so much food on their tight budget. So it was a surprise that as Jack was leaving to catch his flight she gave him a small sandwich to wish him well. "Out of all the thieves that I've known, you have been the best mannered one," she said as they bade him goodbye. Just like that, Jack left his two good friends, the only ones he had, and headed towards America and hopefully a demon to slay.

The flight to America was uneventful except this time there was no skinny accountant sitting next to him. The accountant from the first flight did happen to be sched-uled for that same one but upon seeing Jack boarding the plane he chose to catch the next flight, not knowing that since their last encounter Jack had taken a much-needed bath. As the plane left, Jack felt a pain of regret for leav-ing Ireland and its good people, but he promised to go back someday to see his good friends who had made him feel more alive and human than he had felt for a long time.

The first sight he saw as America came into view was the tall skyscrapers that seemed to be trying to blot out the sky. Metal giants who flaunted their power separate from nature and her beauty, but Jack knew that it had to be that way to accommodate the multitude of people in their honeycombed apartments. When they departed the plane he became instantly aware of that multitude of people in the city, not just by the sheer volume of those moving about, but he could also taste it. The air was thick and overused, regurgitated a few times by other breathers before it came to him. Nature's filters weren't able to keep up with the fumes in the area. Jack was not one that could appreciate the large crowds and busy attitudes of those in the cities, and in some strange way, he was more intimidated by the city's atmosphere than the prospect of fighting a demon.

If he only knew the sights and wonders that the city had to offer, or even tried some of its illustrious food prepared by well-practiced cooks, he may have changed his mind. However, that did not come to pass for as soon as he could, he boarded the next flight to his hometown to start his search for the trouble-causing unicorn.

The strangest thing was that ever since he left Mort's, he never felt any sense of dread that one would expect to have when setting out to fight a demon. He felt quite the opposite and I dare say that he was happy at the prospect of it.

Once the plane landed in Illinois, he hitched a ride from a kindly old gentleman in a truck to his old home. A few times the elder man tried to strike up a conversation but Jack, not being one for conversation, didn't say much in response. After a few dull attempts, their conversations ceased completely. It didn't matter to Jack, who had taken to watching the urban environment slowly disappear, as they drove farther into farm country.

Jack was not particularly fond of the idea of going where his happy life ended and this dismal life he now knew began, but he knew that he had to start his search somewhere and this was the best place. During a quick stop, he grabbed a newspaper to see if any new reports of strange deaths had occurred, but to his dissatisfaction the only deaths were murders by other hostile human beings. Sometimes he wondered if humans, not demons, were the more destructive players in people's troubled lives.

As they drove closer and closer to Jack's place, he could feel a wave of nervousness creep into him like slow trickle from a hole in a dam that threatened of something greater to come. His nervousness must have been obvious as the driver asked multiple times if Jack was all right, to which Jack would respond with a simple, "Yep." But in truth, he was not feeling all right, as the roads became familiar to him, his memories of the past came hurling back, each memory with greater force than the previous one. At last, when the kind truck driver dropped him in front of his old house and took off, Jack could not hold it in any longer and broke down in tears from the wave of emotions that overtook him.

He stayed there in front of the desolate house until his tears dried up. After a while of uncertainty, Jack made his way to the house. Entering the structure was not difficult, for its front door was open, hanging on one hinge. The inside did not fare much better. Due to its leaky roof, the floor was soft, which had cracked the walls even more than when Jack left. It was amazing to Jack just how much it had fallen into decay, as if it, too, felt the ruin of destruction of the family it once harbored. The house looked just as Jack felt inside: empty and destroyed.

Jack moved on to Abigail's room but looking in, he saw that it was destroyed by some wild party long past. He felt sickened in his heart that they dared tarnish her memory or disrupt her space by tearing up the walls, smashing the windows, and ripping up the floor boards to make a hole to the first level where a mound of trash now lay. But that was not the worst of it, for on the walls they had drawn signs of the devil. If they only knew what happened in that very place, they may have thought better of it. Sickened, Jack left the house, trying to put some distance from him and that place, but what he saw still haunted him as he cursed their disrespect for his daughter's memory.

As he hurried away from the house he came to the corral where his precious daughter met her ill fate. Where it was least expected, he saw something beautiful, and it gave him some peace. Resting against the spot where he found Abigail's body was a fresh bouquet of flowers that his neighbor Timothy had put there. Bless that kind-hearted neighbor, who took especially good care of the area and provided it with fresh flowers whenever he could.

As one could expect, this brought more tears to his eyes but unlike the previous ones these were in appreciation of the kind soul. He looked towards Timothy's distant house with a thankful glance. Strengthened by the kindness towards Abigail's memory, he turned back towards his own decrepit house that loomed silently, beaconing wretched creatures to come to it, so Jack did.

Stepping back inside, Jack, who was weary and worn, came into the living room. Like the rest of the house, it was trashed; however, one piece of furniture that seemed to more or less survive the rampage of destruction was his lonely ripped recliner. Its color had faded considerably and a hunting knife could clearly be seen gouging its back, but it was usable.

Jack slowly approached the chair like a man would a strange animal. Remembering the countless nights that he sat intoxicated in this chair, he gripped the handle of the knife. Half wanting to plunge the knife deeper into the chair, he remembered his old self, drunken with despair, while Abigail was left alone to face the hardships of the world, without the father's comfort she deserved after her mother's passing.

Cursing his old self, he slid the knife out of the chair. It was a simple knife, plain in design with some rust on the handle, but its blade was strong. Jack sat in his recliner that seemed to welcome him with an old friend's embrace and threw dust from its seat as if in celebration of their reunion. Jack slowly took out a small pouch that he had prepared in Ireland and slipped out a bottle. Opening it, he took out a paste of smashed clover and wiped it on the blade. This was the knife's new meaning: to be the means of an end. He swore that it would not rest again until it was dug deep into Summer's heart. He sat in the chair pondering this until late in the night, not getting much sleep

for the anticipation of the half moon tomorrow. He waited
in the silent house that was a grim reminder of what happened, and inspiration strengthened his resolve.

As the moon rose on the second night, Jack was prepared with knife sheathed and an ax in hand, both smeared
with the clover paste. He took to a secluded patch of woods
outlining the farm and waited on a small hill overlooking
the flat woods. His pulse beat with anticipation, with every
sound, he turned with an agitated want of battle. The night
smelled of a coming storm, and the air was thick with mosquitoes but still he held his stance. So intent was he to see
his foe that a tornado couldn't have budged him from his
perch. Only when the sun rose and shone high in the sky
did he at last get up.

"Didn't want to show yourself, I see," he said in an
annoyed tone. "Just what I would expect from a coward
that preys on children." With that, he made his way back to
the house which would be his homestead while he hunted
the unicorn or until another lead sent him elsewhere.

"He didn't show himself," he said to himself.
"Why? Did I get the phase of the moon wrong? Yes! That
must be it! How do I find out which moon it is?" He looked
in a shattered mirror and seeing how bloodshot his eyes
were, became aware that he needed sleep. Until he was certain what phase of the moon the unicorn would appear, he
would wait up every night in the woods until his accursed
foe finally showed himself.

Wait he did: for a full six half moons he waited

in those woods for Summer to appear. He waited through storms, he waited through the mosquitoes that came in droves for their free meal, he waited in the silence of the night when even the crickets and frogs were asleep. Every night he waited, but never once did Summer appear. Then during one of those nights when everything was quiet and Jack was in deep thought he got up. Looking into the night sky that shown brightly with the miracles of heaven, he gave a heavy defeated sigh and headed towards the house.

Setting his shotgun, that he procured the previous week through mischievous means, against the wall, he sat down onto his chair in deep thought about the whole ordeal until the realization hit him. Summer was not coming; the unicorn was a myth after all. He started chuckling to himself until it came to a full roar then dissipated into tears. Imagine what his wife Rachel or Abigail would have thought. How ashamed of him they must be!

"What am I supposed to do, Rachel?" he cried, dropping to his knees. "What am I supposed to do? Tell me." Wiping the tears from his eyes only to have them fill up again, he looked towards the sky for some sign. "Why did you leave? I'm not strong enough…the burden is too great." He struck the wall next to him, cracking it even further. "It should have been me!" he screamed in anguish into the echoes of the empty house. "God, you should have taken me!" He could barely breathe through his tears and what little air he received came out in a wheezy sob.

His life was wasted on foolish searches and past

dreams of the happiness he once had. Now all he had was regret; there was nothing, simply nothing for him. No family, no house, and no revenge; it was all gone.

"This world, this miserable world, filled with misery, avarice, destruction, and ruin. What a worthy place for me it has truly become. A living Hell, for my pitiful life, cut off from those I love, doomed to chase shadows of false happiness as the night swallows what little left I have. I truly let them down." He turned his eyes once more towards Heaven, then gave one last apology to his family and I suspect to himself before the exhaustion of his emotional plight overtook him and carried him into a deep sleep.

When he awoke, he neither spoke nor cried, but he grabbed what little he had and walked out into the sun. Without ever looking back at his dreary old house, he began down the dirt road. Jack knew not where he was going or even what day or season it was. He didn't care; such worries for him disappeared long ago. He just wanted space between him and the foul memories of the past. To wander this world until the Lord in pity called him up was the path that now lay before him, to be a rouge in this cruel world, a stranger in an unfamiliar land was his calling and to him, it made sense. These ideas would be frightful to many a man, but to Jack it felt right and prepared in his heart he was to take on the role of a wanderer.

Now many would see this decision as a means to escape, from bad memories or his ill lot in life, and would even dare to scoff at him for taking such a cowardly role, but such things, given time, can work into a higher plan. For Jack, after many months of traveling the countryside came upon a pub. It was a humble pub tucked amongst the overgrowth of dirty apartments and littered streets. The sign above the pub was old, rusted, and dreary, but its faded image hinted of brighter times when it once showed itself proudly amongst the street as if proclaiming to those passing bye of its grand stature. Upon it read The Golden Ladybug and although it was faded, the words still held their sharp brilliance wrapped in lacy art.

The exterior of the pub had chipped art and broken decorative plaster that showed of a time when such things were important to this neighborhood's atmosphere. In its cracked plaster were carvings of ivy, trees, flowers, lady-bugs, and butterflies, all in a brilliant display, seemingly looking up towards the bright sun on the top of the building's exterior. Much was cloaked under vegetation and moss, but surely in its prime this must have been a majestic pub indeed.

Jack opened its old thick door that creaked in greet-ing before he slipped into the dark smoke filled place. The interior was much like the outside, with plaster ceilings filled with fantastic quaint designs that nicely accommodat-ed the building's old wood floors and the broad stage that was now seldom used. He focused his attention to the bar that was etched in faint gold paint and went up to it, where he was greeted by a skinny bartender who had a very large mustache that seemed to have a life of its own by the way it moved when he talked. He ordered a drink and nursed it down while he curiously watched the others in the bar. Around one of the wooden tables, people were playing an intense poker game that Jack predicted would soon erupt into violence. Two tables from them was an old man with a trucker hat who was busy flirting with a young lady.

Jack's attention was quickly drawn to two drunken men in the far corner. Although they were some distance away, their slurred voices could be heard quite clearly. There were just the two men, one was average in size but well built, with a worn face that showed hard labor. The second was a small portly fellow who was well-groomed, but his features were aged beyond what they should have been. This was perhaps from years of nagging by the aggressive wife that he now rambled on about to the larger man and how it was getting harder to escape her clutches to the solitude of the bar, or what he called his oasis.

"I know it's hard," said the bigger man taking another swig, "but you just need to stand up for yourself. Nobody deserves to be henpecked to death. It's unnatural."

"I tried," the smaller one replied, agitated. "God knows that I tried. She just won't listen! She says she understands but immediately switches the subject to something that she thought I did wrong. Day after day, hour after hour, I'm on pins and needles never knowing what will set her off; I can't take it. Something has to change."

"Then tell her to stop! You have been telling me that you would for years." He leaned in, pressing the issue.

"Is she really that scary that you would rather be miserable than stand up for yourself?"

The little man said nothing but stared into his drink in defeated shame. "You don't understand," he finally replied. "I love her, I really do, but even if she could see what she's doing, she couldn't change, even if she wanted to."

"So you're just going to suffer, then?" The little man did not respond to this but looked away as if he wished to escape the conversation. Seeing his friend was done talking, the bigger man gave a grunt of disappointment, "Well it could be worse, you could have a daughter who outright hates you."

"How is Jenny doing?" The shorter man replied, thankful for the sudden change of subject.

"She's fine. In fact she has the top grades of her third grade class." He hung his head in sorrow. "Doesn't want anything to do with her father, but she's fine." The smaller man tried to assure him that it was just a phase that kids go through and that it would pass, but it didn't seem to cheer the man up any. "I just wish I knew what to do. She keeps drifting away more every day, I'm afraid that I am going to lose her."

"You're not going to lose her."

"Do you know what she told me yesterday?" he asked in which the smaller man shook his head no. "She told me that she wished I was dead. I had to work late and missed her recital and she now wishes me dead, can you believe that?"He took another drink and became quieter and more somber to a point where Jack really had to listen to hear what he was saying. "She is right though. I am a failure. I work myself to death, miss her activities because of it, and still can't afford to put bread on the table. If it wasn't for the church, we would have starved long ago."

"Give it time," his friend tried to reassure him. "One day when she realizes what you sacrificed for her and how hard you worked to give her a decent life, she will forget all about any recitals you might have missed."

"You may be right," he admitted, "but by that time even if she forgets about the recitals she will still have taught herself to hate me. I just don't know what to do." He looked at his friend seriously. "Do you think I am a good father?"

His friend quickly replied yes and gave several good reasons why he knew he was; they were true, too.

It was fascinating to Jack that this man who obviously faced many hardships in his life could be brought to such a state of desperation by such a small and fragile thing, but it did show the love that the father truly had for his daughter. He, out of all people, knew just how much a child can affect a parent's life. Looking out a dirty window into the night sky he thought about his own struggle from losing a daughter and why this man was so terrified at the thought of it.

Jack pondered this until another question brought him out of his thoughts.

"She still hasn't fully recovered then?"

"No," the larger man replied to the smaller one. "The sickness comes in spurts. But like I said, she was able to go back to school yesterday so I think she's fine. She keeps telling us that she's feeling better. The Mrs. doesn't believe it, but I think it's true." He leaned in closer, "Personally, I think she's just having anxiety attacks over a quiz. You know how she is."

The smaller man nodded in agreement. He knew far too well that Jenny got sick when she was anxious. The shoes that he had to throw away after being covered with vomit when he went to see the school pageant were testament to that. "You know," he replied with a mischievous tone, "it could be a boy problem." The larger man leaned back as if he was just punched but quickly replied like any protective father would, that that better not be the case and gave all sorts of reasons why. "Come now, my friend," he said, pressing the subject, "you can't tell me that she doesn't have any guy friends?"

"The only guy friend that she has is an imaginary one," the taller man replied defensively and pointed his finger not so steadily, "and he is imaginary."

"Imaginary?" The short man chuckled, not thinking Jenny to be the kind of girl that would play such games. "What's his name?" The taller one thought for a moment before he answered that his name was Summer. At this Jack gripped his glass tightly not able to believe what was just stated, but he said nothing, listening intently. "How do you know that it's not just a boy that she says is imaginary?"

the smaller one pressed, now having fun at the taller one's expense, "He could be real." The taller one shook his head no. Jack could feel the blood rush from his face as a cold sweat began. A mixture of emotions began to swell inside him as he listened for what he knew was to come.

"Of course he's imaginary," the taller one replied. "He's a unicorn."

The smaller man never got out his next words, for at the utterance of unicorn, Jack's grip became too much for the poor glass he was holding and it shattered, spilling its contents. An enraged Jack leapt up with such a scream of frustration that it demanded the attention of every person in the bar.

Jack stood, blood dripping from his hand, giving a glare of a Wildman at the men who just shattered his new life. During the past few months as a wanderer, Jack had managed to put most of the past behind him and only seldom gave thought to his old life or his hunt for the demon unicorn called Summer. He had thought himself free of it, but now, he was back. Back in that dark dungeon of his soul that he knew all too well, where turmoil and misery were abundant and threatened to devour his being. He knew that escape from this doom was impossible, and with that revelation, he stormed out of the bar into the night cursing his ill fate.

The whole bar watched as Jack stormed out of the bar. "What is his problem, Dale?" one of them asked the bartender when Jack was well out of earshot.

The bartender stared at the door. "I don't know," he admitted, "but he did pay his tab," he continued, looking back towards the people in the bar. "Something I wish would happen more often."

It was a strong hint and the others in the bar quickly looked away as if they suddenly remembered something very important elsewhere. The bartender grunted and made his way to retrieve the mop.

Gloomy, that was the only way to describe the night air. Whether the air was like this because of the humidity that had already begun to create a slight fog around the buildings, or the stuffy feeling from the buildings being too close to each other, I could not say, but it can be said with utmost certainty that it was a gloomy night.

The streets were worn and uneven. The people dressed in shabby stained rags moved with a slow emotionless pace, as if they were lonesome spirits and doomed to wander for eternity as such. They meandered between the old abused cars on the street with only the light of the moon for guidance. The old lamp posts of the street had long been out of commission.

One particular lamp which had no globe, being shot out years ago, shown with a pitiful display of chipped paint and rust that seemed to slide from its head as tears from a face. It was indeed a pitiful sight to behold, but even though, its story was a sad one of ruin. It was nothing like the story of the man below it that it now seemed to stare at with wondrous pity.

Jack mumbled to himself as he slowly made his way in a heavy pace below the old lamp. Jack was indeed in a pitiful situation. He wanted nothing else than to forget what he had heard and to flee the area with all haste. But something deep in him held a tight grasp on the idea that he had to stay and find the meaning behind what the man had said.

"Why must I stay? We both know how this ends," Jack desperately pleaded with himself. "Why not go? Live what little life we have in peace." The same feeling told him that running was not going to end well and would not solve his problems but prolong them.

"Why me?" he mumbled to himself. "Why is this all happening to me? Why was I given a family only to have it ripped away so violently in the end? It would have been better to never have one at all and be safe from this heartbreak."

The voice asked him if he truly believed if it would have been better to not have had a family at all and to have lived his whole life as he did now. Jack made no answer, for he knew that his inner voice was right.

Jack, losing his strength, leaned against the lamp post. To have never felt his wife Rachel's warm embrace, to have never heard his daughter's soft giggles, or to never have the chance to hold her in the hospital as he and Rachel looked upon their child with silent happy tears was too much to bear. Even if it did end so abruptly and terribly, his life with his family was truly a blessing. He slid down the post as its rusty paint chips flaked off "What a fool I am," he thought to himself. He put the thought of ever wishing such a thing from his mind.

For the first time in years, he was grateful that even though he never deserved it, he was given such a blessing, even if it was for such a short time. He slowly got up, strengthened by this. "He truly does work best in weakness," he muttered. He looked towards the bar just as the taller man who told of his daughter's imaginary friend came out with the smaller man. Jack's path was laid out before him and he knew it. With a submissive nod he began to follow the two men.

The two men were full of spirits and never noticed him as they stumbled along the road towards their homes. In fact, Jack could have been in the very midst of them and the two men wouldn't have noticed, such was their demeanor from the overconsumption of drink. But kept his distance, Jack did, as the two men came to an intersection and stopped. They stood and talked for a good while about what was discussed in the bar: sports, and other fond memories including a new one of the crazy man who they thought was going to kill them before he stormed out of the bar.

After a few more jokes, some of personal matters, which only good friends can make, they split up, and each took a different road towards his home. The little man staggered down the dark street, humming a fine country tune which was really not bad for a man who could barely feel his tongue. Jack, paid him no attention but cautiously followed the taller man down the street.

The taller man, who was having about as much luck in following a straight line as his friend was, slowly made his way up a windy road. They walked past old houses worn and in disrepair, past rusty mailboxes and cluttered lawns. They traveled to the outermost part of town where next to a secluded patch of woods. There stood a house.

The house was simple and matched the others in age. It stood with steep roof that Jack suspected, as he peered at it through the dark, was covered in clay shingles. The house seemed to have been a farmhouse at one time and had a weather beaten barn in back. The fields around it were hardly recognizable as such under the overgrowth. The house displayed recent repairs some of which were creative, as if their designer didn't have time to give their designs more thought. The barn, though, was uninhabitable caused by a true act of ignorance of its desperate plea for repair. Never once did the barn receive any care from the taller man, who still paid it no heed as he made his way to the house's door.

As the man entered his house with the grace one might expect from a drunken man, Jack pulled out his ax and knife and prepared them for the night, then sat down with his shotgun in his lap and waited. What Jack was waiting for, he did not truly know, perhaps for Summer to attack suddenly from one of the trees. He was prepared for such a fight. However, in his heart he knew that he could not find Summer on his own, not without her. The other reason he was here besides revenge was the little soul he needed to save from a grim fate.

He waited until late in the night, long after the other nocturnal animals ceased their hunts and calls in the dark. The sky now shone with careful vigor the stars above, which twinkled with the brilliance of a diamond's sparkle on a black canvas. He waited still, until at last he saw what he knew and was afraid that he would see: a little girl climbing out of her window and disappearing into the woods as if late for something very important. Jack quickly proceeded to follow the girl, determined to finally meet his foe, but fate, however, deemed it necessary that he should fail. As Jack entered the outskirts of the woods, bent on finding Summer, he did not pay careful attention to his footing, so it is of no surprise that in his haste he slipped on a rock, hit his head, and knew no more until the sun woke him.

It took a moment for Jack to realize what had happened, but once he did, such cursing ensued that a sailor would be put to shame. How could this have happened? Why? When he was prepared in his heart and mind to finally face the nightmare that plagued his soul? He laid there furious with his stupidity. What did he expect to happen running through the dark woods, like an overeager child, to fight a demon? He should have had more caution in his step. It is a serious affair after all; a child's life hangs in the balance. A child's life! Is she still alive? Was it a half moon last night?

Quickly, Jack jumped up alarmed by these questions and ran to the window that the girl snuck out of last night. There, to his relief, she laid with a thermometer in her mouth. The child was clearly in distress with beads of cold sweat upon her forehead. It was a sweet face and full of innocence. It was hard to imagine she could utter such words as her father reported last night and truly knew their meaning.

Jack quickly ducked out of view as the girl's door opened. A calm, sweet voice which could only be the girl's mother was soon heard and even though Jack did not see the care the mother was giving her sick child, her voice told him how much she truly adored and loved her little girl.

Jack leaned against the house, relieved beyond all measure that the child was still alive. If Summer truly existed and took the girl because of his stupidity he could have never forgiven himself.

He gave a slight laugh as he slid down the wall. Throwing back his head to look at the clear sky, he noted how lucky they both were and while he was unconscious laying on the ground that Summer did not pay a visit to him.

Looking back down, his eyes rested on the woods. Even during the day, they seemed dark. Only a little light managed to show through the tree's thick canopy before it was choked out by the thick underbrush.

No wonder Jack tripped! With the clutter of stones and dead tree limbs, it was amazing that the child even made it through such a barricade. Jack got up, and with a final glance towards the window, he made his way cautiously to the woods. He soon found a path that the child must have taken the previous night and made his way in, disappearing into the menacing woods.

Luckily for Jack, the ground was quite moist, and although he was no skilled tracker, he could make out the little footprints of the small girl quite clearly. Deeper into the woods they lead, and as the trees grew closer, making it hard to maneuver, Jack felt it necessary to take out his gun, just in case something was there. Deeper still he went, until the footprints lead through a small hedge of thorns, much to Jack's discomfort, and entered into a small clearing of straggly grass.

There the footprints stopped. They were sunk deep as if the child had stood there a long time. Looking back at the tracks, he noted that the ones heading back to the house were different than the ones coming to the clearing. The tracks were staggered, almost in a drunken fashion. Jack wasn't sure of what the tracks meant, but he had his theories on the matter, considering the girl's sudden sickness. Jack put these ideas to the back of his mind. What was really important to him was finding any clues of Summer's presence.

Shotgun in hand, Jack searched the area. The trees looked normal, as did the nuts hanging delicately from their branches. There was nothing hiding in the thick bushes surrounding the clearing. No animal tracks on the ground; not even a sign of a squirrel could be found, let alone a unicorn. Even the insects seemed to give the clearing a wide berth and did not dare venture into its domain, which was fine by Jack. He had more encounters with mosquitoes during his nightly hunts than he cared to remember. Everything in the clearing seemed quite normal, but those footprints… Something was happening here and Jack was determined to find the answers.

Perplexed, Jack started his slow march out of the woods, still on high alert for anything that might be stalking around. But there was nothing; not even a bird could be heard. It was as if all life had fled from the woods, leaving the dank trees alone with only piles of moldy leaves on the ground for company. It really was an unpleasant patch of woods, and he was glad when he left it.

As he came out of the woods, he stopped by the girl's window again to make sure she was still all right. Jack knew that hanging around the house was dangerous and that he was indeed trespassing, but he had to see the girl once more to make sure her condition had not worsened. The mother was not there, but the girl could be clearly seen sleeping peacefully or as peacefully as a sick child could. It gave him hope that perhaps this time it would be different. That this time she will live and Summer will die. If he could save this little girl from the demon that he had been hunting and save her parents the heartbreak from losing a child, then maybe he could finally be able to truly move on with his life.

Slowly and quietly, he moved away from the window with new determination to save the child. He set up watch in a small brush pile far from the house and away from any possible traffic and waited. The brush hid him from any prying eyes, but it did not obstruct his own view of the surrounding area, especially the girl's window. He needed to make sure she couldn't sneak out without him seeing, otherwise he could not protect her.

There he waited, knowing that the girl was the key to finding Summer and although he did not enjoy the idea of using the girl to lure out a demon, his hatred of Summer was stronger and he was willing to allow it.

There he waited throughout the day and into the night, ignoring his hungry stomach and parched lips. He knew and was afraid that if he left to quench these desires that the girl could slip out the window without him knowing and all would be lost, so he stayed at his post, keeping a sharp eye on the house and the woods next to it. Even when the flies came in swarms around his head, he still did not move. He was determined not to fail.

The sun dropped and after a sweet kiss on the Earth in the form of a fiery sunset, as if wishing the Earth goodnight, it was gone. Looking up towards the heavens as the night sky began to glow; Jack noted that the moon, loosely dressed in her cloak of light, was close to a half moon.

Whether it was waxing or waning, he did not know. It was a good night where the night breeze gently brushed his cheeks with its soft touch of chilled air, making his eyes heavy and body lax. Hours passed before the father came home in an intoxicated manner. No wonder he couldn't put bread on the table! Most of their money must have gone to the bar for him to come home in such a manner every night.

The door opened and closed. He heard a few muffled sounds of the drunken man and his wife sternly talking. Then there was silence. The lights turned off, leaving Jack to the mercy of the night's dim light. Looking towards the child's window again, he waited in silent patience until the night began to show signs of giving way to the bright sun.

Something was wrong. Jack could feel it. The demon hunted at night and it was becoming day. The window for Summer to feed was slipping away, and yet he saw no movement of the girl slipping out the window. Jack sat and pondered this until an alarming thought came to him. Maybe the girl slipped out another part of the house and he did not see her leave!

Jack hastily made his way to the girl's window and peered in. Thanks to a little light next to the bed, he could see the faint shape of the girl asleep on the bed. Relieved, he moved away. After a moment's hesitation of what to do, he looked towards the woods. Perhaps Summer was in there now waiting for the girl, not knowing that her sickness kept her in bed, but if he was waiting it won't be for long. Day was coming fast, and if Jack wanted to rid the world of the unicorn, he needed to be faster.

Jack bolted into the woods, gun drawn for a fight. The shotgun shells that he prepared had lead in them mixed with his special paste of clover, which he was fully confident could do the job of killing Summer. If not, he still had his knife and ax. There was no way that he was going to let Summer escape. If he was in the clearing, Jack was going to find him and bring the loathsome fiend to justice, for Abigail, himself, and all other lives the demon destroyed.

Deeper Jack ran, breaking the limbs of plants that caught his clothes as if trying to hold him back. Perhaps they knew his intent and wanted to prevent the confrontation between him and Summer. Jack, though, would have none of it and ripped through the woods with speed, strength, and an unshakable resolve to confront the demon, until at last he found himself in the midst of the clearing.

The clearing was now faintly lit by the sun's rays. He looked around but could see nothing, not even a trace of the creature was there. With an agitated scream, Jack fell onto his knees. He missed him! How could this have happened? Why was he not there? It was infuriating. Every time he thought he would find his foe and exact his vengeance, he did not. It was as if some being was having fun at his expense, making him chase shadows that could never be caught. Looking up in silent prayer, Jack asked why, when he was so willing, that he could not find his prey and end its reign of terror once and for all.

After a while, in silent disappointment, Jack got up

and left the clearing. The sun was high in the sky as Jack made his way back. He took a quick rest at the brush pile but was soon awoken by a stomach that, tired of its hunger being ignored, cramped up and led Jack towards some much needed nourishment. Jack soon found a small tavern and though it was dirty and shown signs of age, it provided him with a very satisfactory meal. With stomach filled and thirst quenched, Jack began to get up to leave but was stopped by a very old gentleman who decided to pay for Jack's meal.

"I'm Herb," the old man said to Jack, peering slyly at him through his spectacles. He tipped his round cap in greeting, then sat gracefully next to Jack and ordered them both a drink.

Jack stared at the man, perplexed by his generosity. "Have we met before?" he finally asked.

"Course not," the man happily replied, taking a swig "It's a lovely day, don't you think?" the man continued. Jack, not sure what to say, answered that it was and continued staring curiously at the man. They sat in uncomfortable silence until the man, Herb, finished his drink. "There's nothing like a good drink to get the heart started in the morning," the man finally said. Jack grunted in response.

"What is it you want?" Jack eventually asked the old man.

"I don't think that it's about what I want, my friend," the man answered with a trace of seriousness in his happy tone. "It's more about what you want."

"What are you babbling on about?" Jack asked, now certain that this man was trying to sell him something. What it was, he had no clue, but his guard was up now and his tone became harsh. Herb, however, didn't seem to notice and replied that if Jack wanted to know, to simply follow him. He then left the tavern. Jack didn't know what to do. The conversation was short, and suspicious on all levels, but something deep inside told him to follow the man. Since he had nothing else to do, he did.

Up and down winding streets littered with all sorts of trash, he followed the man, who seemed to be taking the scenic route to wherever he was going. Their pace was not a fast one as the man worked skillfully with his cane to climb over the uneven terrain that at one time could have been called a sidewalk. Looking around and noticing that the area was becoming more desolate around them, Jack decided to ask where exactly they were going.

"To my place," the old man replied, not even bothering to turn around and look at Jack. If he had done so, he would have seen a very large, agitated man with hands clenched, looking around expecting to be jumped. If somebody was foolish enough to try to mug Jack, they would meet his knife's cold steel and his gun's spray of lead, of that he was sure. However, none of this came to pass, and as Herb said, he led him to a rundown house, or, more accurately, a shack. It was big enough for a person to sleep in and keep dry from the rain, but it could not boast of its size by any means. Even its door was smaller than the ones Jack was used to, and he had to duck to enter.

They were on the outskirts of town next to an unused piece of farmland and abandoned houses. In fact, the only building that seemed to have any use in this part of town was the greenhouse next to Herb's shack. The shack was the smaller of the two structures.

"Please, make yourself comfortable," Herb told Jack. Jack looked around, found a little stool, and propped it against the wall. He took a seat keeping his eyes fixed on the old man the whole time. Jack usually wasn't so distrustful, but the manner in which the man approached him in the bar told him that he knew that he was supposed to be there. Something about the situation unnerved him and chilled him to the bone. He was not scared of the man nor did he think ill of him. There was just something odd and unnatural about their meeting that he could not figure out.

The furnishing in the shack was sparse. There was a bed, a small round table with two chairs around it, and a old fashioned stove that had something simmering on it. The toilet was tucked in the far corner and quite exposed. There were no curtains around it or barrier of any sort, which made Jack think that the old man lived by himself. There were no pictures or decorations on the wall except for a single wooden cross that was well-cared for.

The old man brewed some tea and handed a cup to Jack who accepted it but did not drink. "Why did you want me to come here?" Jack asked when the man sat down.

"I came because I was not busy and curious about what you had to say," he continued, "but I will be very busy tonight and will not stay much longer. Tell me what you have to say, or I'm leaving now."

"Leaving to fight a demon," Herb replied.

Jack dropped the cup, shattering it, and stared dumbfounded at the old man.

"Don't look so surprised. Why did you think I brought you here? It was surely not to give you tea. I told you that I can give you what you want, and that is a tool to complete your task."

This was the last thing that Jack expected to hear this old man say, and it took him totally off guard. How did the man know so much? He had never seen him before, nor did he know any way that the man could have guessed at his intentions. So many questions and fears came to mind, but he could not utter a single one. The old man just sat there studying Jack's expression, to watch his reaction to what he was instructed to tell him. "How?" Jack finally managed to utter. His brain raced frantically with questions and that was all he could manage to say.

"I had three dreams," the man replied. "The first dream was of a strong man with arms like cedar and the heart of black gold. A heart that seeks justice, but to those around, the actions he takes, although they be good, seem to be that of darkness. The man stood upon the weeds with great sadness as his heart was taken by the pale demon cloaked in the brightness of night. Terrible it is, upon the Earth, for in the demon's eyes, I saw its lust for fresh souls which it greedily devours. This creature has many names, but its actions are that of a Cilack which is well known to me."

The man shifted his weight and continued his story. "The second of the three dreams was of the same man in the pastures of green seeking the demon, with hatred in his eyes that leapt out like fire and destroyed everything around except the path he desired. However his foe was hidden from him until the allotted time that they shall meet. In the third dream, I saw the same man in the tavern, the same one we meet in, and a voice spoke to me. It said, "Look upon the man that has fought with demons of sorrow but has not swayed from his path. He hunts the demon of your family but look: his tools are wrong, rusted with ignorance and rushed haste and for this reason their meeting has been stalled." 'What would you have me do?' I asked the voice, and it replied, "Teach him of the leaves and all that you know, for the time is drawing near for the soul he wishes to protect. For soon I shall bring justice to the souls that call out to me from the stomach of the pale steed!"

The man stopped and looked at Jack intently. "The man I saw in my dreams was you and your plight has been revealed to me. You know by whom. However, something else was revealed to me, that if you continue you will be required to sacrifice your life."

– CHAPTER FIVE –

LIGHT OF THE NIGHT

Jack sat there, digesting what was just said to him. The story was hard to believe and he didn't even know where to begin. Herb made it quite clear that fighting Summer would be his end, but as Jack told Mort long ago, he was willing to die if it meant the end of Summer. "So," Jack began, looking at the old man with more humility than before, "the creature, it was hidden from me?"

"You have a powerful ally on your side," Herb replied. "One that has been keeping you from finding your foe." After a slight nod to himself, Herb leaned in closer. "This was done so we could meet."

"But why?" Jack still could not believe what was happening and thought he could at any moment wake from this strange dream. But this was no dream and no accident that these two should meet.

"You have the wrong leaves of three," Herb simply replied. "If you fight the Cilack now it would be as if you were fighting a lion with a twig." Grabbing his cane, Herb slowly got up from his chair, joints creaking.

"I thought that the clover was a sacred plant," Jack replied defensively. "All my research has told me that the plant was a sacred one."

"It is, but it is not *the* sacred plant!" Herb looked up as if remembering something from his past. "My family has been plagued by the same demon as you are now, so in a way your journey is connected to my own. My grandfather was taken by a pale demon many years ago when I was a young lad. I saw it, the horse with a horn on its head." He turned towards Jack, who stared back, eyes wide and fully listening to the man's story. "My family had a name for the creature that attacked him. They called it a Cilack. Like many demons, he eats unfortunate souls, makes them part of himself, and gains strength by doing so. Those poor souls! How horrid of an existence they have, trapped in a body of a demon and tortured by its evil whims! Conscious, but unable to move or speak, they are like a man buried deep in jagged dirt denied the ability to see or even breathe. Horrid, horrid existence! The Cilack, though, is different, special even amongst the demons, for he is allowed to consume not just the wretched souls, but righteous ones as well."

Jack was very alarmed to hear the old man go on like this, and, with every word spoken, he shook more and more. He never thought of what happened to the souls that were eaten and what had happened to his little girl. His anger and fear swelled up at the man's words, "How could such a creature be allowed to exist?!" he demanded.

"Because nobody has been able to kill the pale demon," Herb replied sorrowfully. "Many have tried, including myself, but he is elusive and has taken many lives of many hunters. That's where I hope you will be different. I was told to tell you how to defeat this foe of old, and that's what I intend to do."

Noting that the man knew more than he did on this matter, Jack decided to listen to any advice that he could get. "Tell me, if the clover is not the sacred plant, what is?" The man walked over to his window sill and took a plant off its ledge. With a thoughtful nod, he took the plant over for Jack to see. It was a plant that Jack was very familiar with. Its red stem and three leaves were unmistakable, and it had caused him much trouble in the past, for the plant was poison ivy. "Really?" was all that Jack could say. The thought of a weed being a sacred plant with the power to take down a demon was hard to believe.

"Yes, the sacred plant is poison ivy, three leaves for the Trinity, and the red stem which is the blood of Christ that connects Earth and God," the old man replied. "As the legend goes, long ago, man was overrun with demons and evil spirits that tortured them day and night, and in their anguish, they cried to the Lord for help. The Lord had mercy on them and created a plant to ward off the evil beings. Its power was very strong and soon the evil fled, but as an act of revenge, the evil spirits placed a curse on man so when they touched the holy plant they themselves would suffer."

Herb put the plant back on the window sill and

continued, "These are the true leaves of three, the ones that are a blessing and curse upon the land. With them, you can pierce the hide of any evil spirit or demon, even one as strong as the Cilack."

"So," Jack said, thinking about what Herb said. "I must find some poison ivy and use it on my blade?"

"Don't do that, nobody should ever do that!" the man replied. "Using real poison ivy is dangerous and may kill you if handled improperly, like it has done too many in the past. My family over the years has   genetically altered a strain of this plant. We found a way to refine it, and I am able to make a safe liquid for you to use because of it. It is just as potent to evil beings as it was before, but through the process it has become safe for humans to handle. I have even been able to make powder from it by a family recipe that took years to perfect."

"Do you have some of this made now?" Jack asked, for he knew that his time with the man was coming to a close if he wished to make it back to the house before nightfall. He had a strange feeling that tonight was going to be different than the others he had faced. "You know that I will need to be back before night if I wish to catch this demon before he takes another soul."

"Yes, I know," Herb replied. "The Half moon is tonight, and the Cilack will be allowed to hunt again." Seeing Jack's surprised reaction he expanded on what he had said. "Every half moon when light and dark's struggle is at its most, the Cilack is allowed to hunt on the poor souls that walk the Earth. According to the tale that my grandfather used to tell us, during this time a strong hunger is put into him and he must eat. To not eat and have his fill is the worst type of torture imaginable for the creature. He enjoys the souls of the living too much, especially the souls of the young." After a quick pause, he continued with a sadder tone than what was usual with him. "Younger souls are not as tainted as older ones and are harder to consume. This means that he must take time to taint and weaken them to make his meal easier to digest."

Once Jack realized what the man had said, his anger flared up. In rage he punched the wall, puncturing its weak plaster. "No," he growled, "that fiend, to befriend my daughter in order to prepare her soul for food, like some type of meat!" He jumped, up kicking his stool over. "He will die a thousand deaths!"

Herb stared at Jack with understanding. After all, the loss of a daughter was bad enough, but then to be told how a creature prepared her soul to be food must be hard to hear. He sat motionless as Jack vented his rage. In truth, Herb had pity on Jack, for he reminded Herb of himself when he was younger and his grandfather was taken by the creature. The anger and hatred that the creature brought haunted him even to this day, but he certainly had more skill in controlling this anger, where Jack obviously did not.

Slowly, Jack's rage dissipated to where he could finally speak again. "Give me the liquid so I may destroy this demon," he growled.

"I will," Herb replied, adjusting his stance in the chair, "but you must calm down before you hunt the Cilack."

"No! My anger shall not be quenched, not until Summer lies dead at my feet!" Jack raised his hand in proclamation. "He will have no defense as I tear into him with my bare hands and smite his body upon the ground for the worms to digest."

"You are a fool," Herb replied harshly. Jack was about to respond to this, but Herb cut him off. "I have seen this creature first hand. I watched it rise from the grass like mist, glowing with power and hate. Quicker than a bird, it moved and overwhelmed my grandfather like a bear would a salmon. Do not underestimate the Cilack." He tapped his cane on the ground in urgency, stressing the importance of his words. "Even with the leaves of three, the creature's fury could not be stopped and now his soul is in the belly of Hell! You must not rush in with an unclear head, for even with all your rage, the demon is stronger still. Its fury is the most terrible sight that one can be unfortunate enough to witness. Unyielding in its hate and malice, it cannot and should not be underestimated. It is a demon fueled by the strength of countless souls. Treat it as such!"

Jack stared at the man. Surprised by his outburst, he had forgotten that the man saw this creature as well, and lost someone dear to its horrible hunger. He stood there until his hot blood had cooled and his breathing became steadier. Herb in turn, stared at him, unmoving, with the patience of one who truly understood. Jack shook his head with dissatisfaction but he was not so blinded by his anger to not see the wisdom in Herb's words. With an agitated grunt Jack picked up the stool and sat back down.

With a nod of satisfaction, the old man got up from the table and motioned Jack to follow. They left the little shack and made their way to the greenhouse beside it. The path was rough and littered with rocky soil that kicked up great clouds of dust wherever they stepped. It was surprising to Jack that the old man could move as fast as he could towards the building on such ground. He seemed to have every inch memorized and didn't even have the need to look down at his steps. Instead, Herb looked at the building with an urgent need, for he, like Jack also wanted to see the demon fall and had rested this hope on Jack.

They soon came to the old door which creaked open with rusted hinges. The building had two rows of skinny carriages that held all types of plants with their two shelf designs. The light fell through the buildings dull yellow wrapping and made the room very hot and humid, forcing Jack to leave his pack and trench coat at the door as they went inside.

"These plants have been in my family for generations," Herb said as he stopped and studied a fern as carefully as a father would a child. Once satisfied with the fern, they quickly moved towards the far end of the greenhouse.

There, tucked under the end of one of the carriages was a worn box. Herb opened it so Jack could see the array of bottles and brown sacks of powder. Herb looked through the box of poorly labeled bottles, some of which had been in there for a long time. Quickly glancing up, Jack noted that in the far corner there was a table filled with glass jars and beakers for measurements. Obviously this man had tampered with the complex and strenuous art of chemistry.

"Here it is," Herb said as he took out a brown bottle of elixir. Opening its cap, he dabbed some of the brown goo onto his finger and inspected it. The concoction did not have a pleasant smell by any means. Truth be told, it took some willpower on Jack's part to stay close to the opened bottle. Herb, however, seemed unaffected by this smell as he studied the paste. Once satisfied of the quality in the bottle, he quickly closed it and gave it to Jack.

"That paste is very good to cleanse houses of bad spirits," Herb said, "but many decided that the smell was worse than the spirits, so I only have the one bottle made." He opened a little sack and procured some white salt-like powder from it. "This powder is also very good and has an extract of the three leaves. I was able to purify it to make it safe for human touch, although I recommend not breathing it."

He gave the sack to Jack, but before letting it go he warned that the demon that attacked his grandfather did so while in the form of mist and the powder might be good to keep on hand, ready to use anytime. "I will put it in my shotgun shells," Jack replied, taking heed of what the man said. Satisfied with Jack's answer, he let the bag go and continued examining the bottles in the box.

After Herb had given all that he could to help Jack, he put the box away. "I cannot stress how quick this creature was when he attacked," Herb began, taking a seat on a brittle chair. "If I can give you any warning, it is that. If you flinch you will be taken. It's as simple and as horrible as that."

The old man really did have a fear of this creature from his own experience and the stories he was told and did not envy Jack's role at all. He was grateful; many years had gone by where there was no sign of the Cilack, and he thought that it really did escape the notice of man. But Jack was living proof that there was still resistance to this horrible creature of night.

It was strange to him that after so many years the creature had decided to come back here, as if it was its territory. He knew that such creatures could move wherever they wanted to and were not bound to any one location or country, but it was still strange nonetheless. He put these ideas to the back of his mind. After all, he was here, and Jack was also here to hunt the creature. That's all he needed to know.

"I am truly thankful for what you are doing," Herb said. "I do wish you the best in your hunt, and wish that I could do more for you, my friend."

"You did more than you know," Jack replied, for not only did he give him the tools that he needed to finally kill Summer, but he had also reconfirmed his belief that such a creature existed. Jack went over to his pack and took out three shells for his shotgun. He carefully scraped out as much of the clover paste as he could from the lead shot and filled them with the powder and paste from the jar. He sealed the shells and held one up to the light to inspect his work. "I will finally have my revenge."

Getting up after his short rest, Herb made his way past Jack, opened the door, and motioned towards the low sun. Jack nodded in understanding. He had a ways to go back to the house and little time to do it. "Keep a sharp eye out," Herb replied. "Do not let your guard down for even a minute. If you do, all is lost."

"I will do what needs to be done," Jack replied, becoming eager to finally confront the nightmare that had haunted him so long.

"I have no doubt of that my friend, but you must keep in mind the power you're going against; you're only a mortal, after all."

Looking back at the old man, Jack gave a respectful nod of understanding and thanks for what the man had done and then left the greenhouse with the speed of a man on a mission and the fear of arriving too late. Watching Jack go, Herb offered a brief prayer for his safety and for him to have strength to accomplish his task. Then with a sigh, he returned to his house, having a fresh hole in the wall to fix.

Down the alleys and up the trashed roads Jack ran, rushing past the taverns which blinked slyly at him with neon lights, trying to beckon him into their rough doors. Determined Jack was, and paid no heed to them as he went his way. No distraction would divert him from the mission that he was given. The little girl's life was on the line.

The night was coming fast, and the moon had already begun to appear, as if signaling Summer's rise. Time was running out for Jack, and he knew it, giving him more speed as he raced against the dark sky towards the house. The heavens soon opened up to a multitude of stars, which there being no clouds, they easily shown their light brightly upon the Earth.

It was a good night, cool and silent, as if the Earth had fallen into a restful sleep and even the creatures of night moved around more somberly than what was usual for them. The only creature that seemed to put any effort into his actions that night was Jack, who rushed towards the house with incredible speed until at last, to Jack's relief, the house came into view.

Jack thanked the Lord as he saw the little girl's room light was still on. Coming to the brush pile, he dropped his pack and caught his breath. He had run most of the way here and the exhaustion from it finally caught up with him as he threw his head back to take deep breaths as his heart steadily came to a normal pulse. He had much to do in a short amount of time. Taking out his knife, he began to generously apply the liquid that Herb gave to him. He did the same with the short ax and stuck it in his belt,

leaving the rest of his pack covered in the brush, for he
didn't need more weight to carry. Jack grabbed his shotgun
and made his way towards the woods where he waited.

The lights in the room went off, but still Jack waited
in silence. Soon the father came, humming to himself,
drunk with the spirits from the bar. If the father had only
known what was going on, he would have had no reason to
hum. Jack pitied him, for the father reminded him of himself. Jack wanted to prevent such heartbreak from touching
this family as it did his and was willing to put his own soul
on the line to make sure of it.

The moon was now very high in the sky and glowed
with a dull brilliance upon the ground, wrapping it in its
mystical light. Darker the night grew and duller the sounds
around the woods became, until at last, in the deepest part
of the night, when all other creatures were asleep, the little
girl's window slowly opened with a creak.

After a moment's hesitation, when the girl was
sure that her parents did not wake up from the sound, she
opened it all the way. Out she timidly came in her pink slip-
pers that matched her pajamas. After a few seconds of looking at the yard as if unsure to go any further, the girl started
to cautiously head towards where Jack was waiting. At first,
he was going to let the girl lead him to where Summer was
waiting, but a feeling in him told him not to do so. After all,
Jack knew where Summer was to appear, and there was no
need to endanger the little girl any further.

As the girl approached the trail in the woods, Jack

stepped out, towering before her. Not even a few feet separated the two of them. The little girl stopped, dead in her tracks, frightened out of her wits by the sudden appearance of Jack, but she did not scream in her fright she had forgotten how to. Jack did not say a word to the girl, but he slowly shook his head for her not to come any further. He then pointed back towards the house, then to her, and back again. With great understanding, the girl bolted back to the house and almost clocked her head as she scrambled through the window frame.

Jack knew that she would not tell her parents for fear of being in trouble for sneaking out at night. He also knew that he had scared the girl enough that she wouldn't try to venture out of the house again tonight. In fact, it would take the girl a while to ever venture close to the woods again. The reason Jack scared the girl in this fashion was because he did not want her in the woods when he began his hunt. After making sure that she had made it back safely into her house, Jack with an ill will then turned towards the woods.

"At long last," he thought in satisfaction staring coldly at the woods, "you shall pay for all that you have done to me, and those from before. You accursed being, I shall personally escort you back to Hell where you belong." Double checking that he had his knife in pocket, that the ax was still loosely looped onto his belt and that the liquid had been generously spread onto both of them, he raised his gun, prepared for what he was to find, and made his way slowly into the woods hoping slay a monster.

The woods were dark, darker than he thought they should be, considering the light the moon and stars gave. More than once he scraped his knees against a rock or tripped over a hidden log. Wishing now that he had brought some form of light with him, he cautiously made his way through the forest. There were no sounds of animals or birds, and even the trees did not make a noise, which was strange, for there was a slight breeze tonight. He felt it before he entered the tree line. The leaves should be moving, if even a little. Looking up, he saw that they were perfectly still, as if holding their breath in anticipation. These woods were just not right; there was an evil in the air that seemed to suck the energy from the area towards some dark purpose.

There was something familiar about this feeling, this pressure, which Jack could not put his finger on. He tried to recall where he felt this pressure before but to no avail. He just couldn't remember. Deeper he went into the woods for he knew the way, even if he couldn't see the path. The heavy pressure that he had been feeling came from ahead, and that's where he needed to go. What was this pressure in the air? He thought and thought on this until at last, he finally knew why it felt so familiar. He had felt this pressure before. It was the same that befell his house before Abigail was taken. The pressure was unmistakably Summer.

How powerful this creature must be, to be able to

feel its presence from such a distance. Herb was right to fear such a creature, a fear that Jack had only just now begun to understand. Summer was not one to be trifled with, that was all too clear. He had to be both cautious and swift to have a hope of surviving, let alone defeating the unicorn. With this in mind, Jack raised his gun and opened his senses for what he knew was to come.

This power, it drew him to it. He felt as if he were a fly being lured by the scent of an insect-eating plant. He realized that this was how the creature called his prey to him, luring children with its intoxicating power. In the pressure Jack thought that he could almost hear singing.

After a while the pressure was lifted, as if its owner had fled. Jack was pondering this as he stumbled into the small clearing. Here the moon's light shone clearly through the break in the tree canopy, giving some light for Jack to see what was around him. He moved cautiously around the perimeter of the clearing looking for his foe, but nothing could be seen. There was no unicorn, not even a hint that one had ever been in the clearing. Jack looked around with a keen eye for Summer. He was not in the trees, not in the air, or in the tall weeds. He wasn't even on the trail…he was nowhere.

With rage, Jack struck the tree next to him, scraping his hands on its hard bark. "Summer, you fiend!" He yelled with fury. "Come out and face me, you coward! The girl is not coming, all that there is, is me." When he received no answer, he kicked the dirt and threw stones into the poor trees, but still there was no sign of his foe. "I knew it," he thought to himself. "The pressure disappeared, Summer has fled. I have failed again." He fell on the ground in grief. Then, looking towards the sky, he gave a cry. "I'm so sorry, Abigail, I failed you, again."

With grief in his heart, he cried upon the ground, watering the blades of grass that eagerly accepted it. He was close, so close that he had actually felt the unicorn's presence, but not anymore. It left, as if not wanting to waste its time with Jack, as if he wasn't worth the trouble. It was an insult; after all that the unicorn had done to him, it thought he was not worth bothering with. How dare it! If he ever got his hands on Summer, he would make him suffer a hundred times over for this insult.

He did everything that he felt he had to do; why was he denied his revenge? The thought crossed his mind that perhaps he should have let the girl go into the woods, but he quickly put this thought aside. If he did find Summer and was overtaken, then the girl would have been defense-less. No, he made the right call. He hated to admit it, but this meant that he would have to continue his hunt for Sum-mer. Perhaps next time he would finally come face to face with his elusive foe.

Somberly, Jack got off his knees, knowing that the path he was to tread would be long and tedious, but he was willing to carry the burden. Taking a long hard last look around the clearing, Jack, with a heavy sigh, started back down the winding trail. The expectation of finding Summer and missing his chance to bring justice for what the fiend had done had broken his spirit.

Slowly, he made his way through the cluttered bushes, unbothered by their thorns that gripped tightly to his clothes. All the brambles in the world couldn't have pierced his scattered mind, which was busy pondering a thousand different questions to no avail. This confrontation, or more appropriately, lack of confrontation had changed Jack. That pressure he felt was not normal. It was as if it was a thread or a thread of threads. It was more than could be explained by a mortal mind. Even from such a brief interaction, he now began to think of the world differently than before, as if it were made up of many strands of lives that made a tapestry. A tapestry of what? Jack did not know, although he did feel that it was still unfinished and not ready to be unveiled. This revelation had to have been brought to him by the overwhelming pressure he felt as he continued through the woods, as if his mind grasped hidden secrets from it. The Pressure! Was it his imagination, or was it slowly coming back?

No, it was not his imagination. The pressure was indeed coming back, and quickly too, but this time he could hear something like a delicate whisper traveling on the winds, moving around him, cloaking his mind within its folds as a spider would a web. It was a beautiful, haunting melody flooding his senses in joyful bliss, mocking him.

"Beautiful soul, tormented soul, why do you look for

me? In the trees tall, rocks strong, you will not find me!" Its voice sang through the air.

Jack raised his gun in preparation, but noting that the woods were too dense to react with any speed, he quickly backtracked towards the clearing. There was something chilling in the voice, something that froze his bones, opened his pores in cold sweat, and scattered his brain with terror. It was a feeling of dread and misery that Jack had never felt before and threatened to tear him down to nothing. He felt as if all hope was lost, but although it was strong upon his senses, he resisted the urge to run from the impending doom that was to come and bravely held his ground.

"Tormented soul, lost soul, delicious you are to me. Headstrong ignorant man, you will not find me!"

The voice sounded again, whispering what Jack thought was in his ears. He turned, expecting to be frightened by the face of Summer, but he was not there. Stumbling into the clearing, he moved his head nervously, determined not to let Summer get the drop on him.

As if enjoying their game, the voice rang out again, *"Lost soul, dead soul, wandering between the trees. Looking still to no avail, you will not find me!"*

Jack cursed himself for wanting to find Summer and wished that Summer had stayed away. "I was a fool to think that I could stand against such a creature," he miserably thought. "Why did he come back though?" The answer was simple: the girl did not come and Jack was there. Herb's warnings had come true. The sudden words of Herb came back to Jack as he remembered him saying, "During this time a strong hunger is put into him and he must eat. To not eat and have his fill is the worst type of torture imaginable for the creature." For this reason, even though Jack was more armed than his usual prey, Summer had come back.

"Dead soul, delicious soul, a buffet to be seen. Here I come to feast on your corpse, for here I be!" At that moment, a light of golden mist came from the tree line and rushed with incredible speed towards Jack.

Jack, seeing this in the corner of his eye, turned and fired, not having any time to aim. The shot sprang through the air with a powdery mist and collided with the creature. Just in time too! Another second and Jack would have surely fell. Herb was right about this creature's speed. It took the speed of a bullet to match him.

The gun's shot stuck directly into the ghostly specter which split around him and landed into the tall weeds just behind. The mist then took shape into a truly beautiful white unicorn which radiated as if reflecting the moonlight and bathed the area with its soft glow. This was him, the creature that had haunted his dreams for so long. He had finally found him, and the truth was, Jack wished he hadn't and was terrified. The pressure around the area was thick and made it hard to stand in the creature's presence. Jack could feel his muscles strain under the sheer power that this creature radiated.

Cleary agitated by the stubbornness of its food, the

creature started to circle poor Jack, studying him. With a stomp of its hoof, Summer rose his head high as if in understanding. It then spoke, but not with its mouth. The voice came from all around like an echo in a deep cave, but never once did the unicorn's mouth move. It stared intently at Jack. *"Clever man, wicked man, your death you now see. For the light of the dark shall not be stopped, even by the leaves of three!"*

A truly horrible feeling the creature radiated from it as it spoke these words. Jack, feeling that the creature's words would unravel his resolve, responded to its comment. He felt that if even for a moment his voice could drown out the horrid sound the creature made, that it would be worth it. "Hmp, you really do speak in rhymes," he managed to reply, through the fear that was in his throat.

"Know you I do not, but it matters not, for you shall soon be mine," Summer replied with a mouthful of malice. *"Now moan in misery and drown in despair, for none can help you now."* He took a step closer, forcing Jack to withdraw. *"Your death shall be swift, but not too quick, such is the penance to pay me now!"*

The creature flared its nostrils and charged at Jack quicker than any beast should have been able to. Quickly, Jack grabbed the ax at his side and swung. He missed and caught a part of its mane that dropped to the ground and disappeared like mist. Dodging the blow, the creature looked back at Jack. Then with a soft glow from its horn, its mane grew back as if it was never damaged. It laughed, a horrible laugh it truly was. *"Hunters of the past I have forced their last gasp, thousands have fell to my song,"* it chimed. *"You shall no different be, and I shall take you with ease, your time here is done."*

With those words, the pressure intensified, making holding the ax or even standing impossible. Down Jack fell onto his knee, unable to stand before the overwhelming strength of the unicorn's power. The pressure he felt was not only attacking him physically but also mentally, as if his very soul was under siege. He tried to stick another shell into his gun, but the creature stomped it to the ground. "Curse you, Summer!" he cried.

The creature looked at him, puzzled at the mention of his name, but soon its expression became that of understanding and recognition. Then in a gleeful tone, Summer spoke again. *"Daughter in despair calls to her father still, shouts flee from my ravaging tongue."*

"Abigail?" Jack managed to speak. "How?"

"Soul that is fresh is now in me meshed, the fate you both now share," Summer replied, pinning Jack down, readying to suck out his soul.

This creature was made of souls. Jack knew that from Herb's description of the Cilack, but it sounded like his daughter was still conscious of what was going on. What a truly horrible existence that must be! Staring fearfully at the unicorn that had begun to drain his energy, he let out a single tear at what he had just learned. Jack could feel his body dying and there was nothing he could do about it. As he stared at the growing abyss of death, he thought he saw a slight glimmer. From what though? It was from the unicorn's horn. Suddenly he understood. Its song, the power that held Summer's body of souls together, it came from the horn! With a last bit of energy Jack struggled against Summer's hold and managed to grab his knife. Then with a stroke that took every last bit of his energy, he severed the horn from Summer's body.

Immediately, Summer stopped and for the first time in the creature's long life he felt fear. He staggered back from Jack, and with a terrible hiss of hate towards the man, Summer fell on his side, dead. Summer, the light of the dark, the pale demon, the Cilack, was at last no more. Jack knew that he was dead because the pressure immediately ceased, letting him breathe easily once more. Soon the creature's body collapsed, dissolving into all the souls it had consumed during its life. There were thousands upon thousands of little bright souls; so many that they blotted out the sky. Jack looked on in wonder as they made their way up towards the heavens, while some unfortunate ones slowly drifted down into the ground. One particular soul brushed against him, kissing his cheek before ascending to heaven, and at that moment he knew that it was his little girl, his little Abigail, who kissed his cheek.

Even with all that he had done and all his failures as a father, he knew at that moment that she didn't blame him for what happened, even though she would have been justified. Instead, all he felt was love from his little girl. He couldn't express his gratitude and love for his little girl, who at that moment put all the troubles in his life to right. All he could do was stare through his tears as he watched her float away.

"Thank you, Abigail," he was finally able to say with a smile.

Jack stared up at the sky long after the souls had vanished in their ascent. His body, drained from the ordeal, welcomed the break. It was over. He finally brought justice for his little girl, but what now? He now seemed to have no purpose. Slowly getting up, much to his body's dissatisfaction, he looked towards the dark woods. Looking back to where Summer fell, he made his way over to the area. Scanning around, he saw there was nothing left of the fiend but the well polished horn lying menacingly on the ground.

Jack fearfully stared at it for a long time, expecting at any moment for Summer to appear from it once again, only to horrify the world with its evil presence. Slowly he bent down and examined it. It seemed lifeless, just an empty shell of a long-dead beast, but when his flesh made contact with the object, a presence flowed into him. It was an evil energy left over from the aura of Summer. As it entered his body it threatened to consume him. He felt the world slip away as he fell into a dark void. Doom was all that he could feel. Helpless he fell to an unknown power. He knew that all was lost, but just as he was about to draw his last breath and succumb to the darkness, a fierce warm light came upon him and brought life back into his body. At that moment he became aware of others, Summer's brothers feeding on the helpless inhabitants of Earth. Taking the knife from the ground, Jack slowly stood up, still clenching the horn in his hand. He now understood. His fight against the darkness had just begun.

"You were right, old man," Jack admitted, remembering the warning that Herb had given him. He looked up at the rising sun that was peeking shyly over the trees, letting loose its warm light, chasing away the shadows around him "I did sacrifice my life. I sacrificed it for another."

– ABOUT THE AUTHOR –

D el Henderson, born and raised in Illinois, enjoys writing, fueling his passion and love for
the noble art of putting pen to paper, or more appro-
priate, keyboard to computer. Diving into pure imagination he has produced works that grip his reader's
minds with mystery and suspense as they are brought
into the fascinating world of fiction.

91555331R00090

Made in the USA
Middletown, DE
30 September 2018